THE STAR-CROSSED PELICAN

The Star-Crossed Pelican

Laura Ruth Loomis

Thinklings Books, LLC
Wickliffe, OH

1

A Problem With the Menu

I'd been on the bridge of my spaceship for five minutes, and it was snowing. "Computer," I said irritably, "what do you think you're doing?"

The computer's voice managed to be blandly efficient and smug at the same time. "Keeping the ship on course, maintaining life support, and answering unnecessary questions for the benefit of biological life-forms."

I heard a snicker from Lola, my first officer, the only crew member on the bridge at the moment. "Bridge" seemed like an overly grand term for a space with two elaborate mechanical chairs (mine and the pilot's), three workstations with regular chairs, and a viewscreen. I still didn't know what half the buttons on my chair were for.

Lola was filling in at the pilot's seat. Like all Venusians, she was surrounded by a colorful aura. Today it was a vibrant pink, which meant she was in a good mood.

I kept my voice level. "Computer, you need to fix the environmental controls. Again."

"But the snow is picturesque. It's whimsical. It's—"

"It's freezing, and it's slippery, and it doesn't belong on a spaceship."

"With all due respect, Captain, maybe it's you who doesn't belong on a spaceship." The snow continued falling.

The computer was unfriendly in general, but it seemed hostile

5

toward me in particular. Actually, technology in general seemed hostile toward me. Floatcars, hair dryers, and kitchen appliances malfunctioned if I touched them. My ex-boyfriend Pietro, an over-rated columnist for the *Galactic Times*, claimed I had a technology jinx. He thought it was funny to call me "Jam-it" instead of Janet.

I hit a button on the arm of the captain's chair. "Martian, where are you?" Martian (yes, he'd be happy to explain at length, that really was his name) was the ship's engineer, and the only one who had any luck reasoning with the computer.

"We're having a snowball fight in the shuttle bay. Hang on, I'm gonna duck behind the—ow!"

After a brief silence, I asked, "Are you all right?"

"Yeah, I think I can stand up. Good thing I don't need the doctor. I almost knocked her out with a snowball, and now she's—"

The button blinked several times, and the connection fizzled out.

Lola turned, pulling her long blonde curls out of her face. Her aura muted the effect of the garish uniform, which was in eight clashing colors. "Personally, I prefer a good swordfight, but snowballs will do in a pinch. The whole crew's been on edge lately." She didn't add *especially you*, but I heard it in her tone. "We're overdue for shore leave. This trip to Cygnus IV can't be over fast enough."

Shore leave sounded heavenly, and our destination didn't have snow. "Can't argue with that."

The ship jolted sideways as a laser blast crackled in front of the viewscreen.

"Damage?" I demanded.

"We weren't hit." The computer sounded amused. "We got caught in the energy wave when lasers hit the shields on the Plutonian."

Lola brought the ship around, and we saw the combatants, a Jupiteran ship and a Plutonian one. I hailed them both. "This is Captain Janet Delane of the GUPPEAS ship S.S. *Cosmic Turkey.*" I skipped the full name of both the organization and the ship, figuring they'd get bored and start shooting again before I finished. "Please identify yourselves."

The Plutonian appeared onscreen first, his gray-green reptilian face scowling. "This is Adequate Leader of Pluto, aboard the ship *Adequate One*. That Jupiteran cut us off, interfered with our sensors, and dumped its garbage in front of us." His antennae writhed indignantly.

"Did you call me *it*?" A bright yellow Jupiteran appeared on the split screen. Jupiterans were shape-shifters, but this one was in their natural form, resembling a four-foot rubber ball with legs and a crude semblance of a face. Jupiterans also had forty-seven genders and a bewildering array of pronouns. My security chief, Nlubglub, was a *they*, and became dangerous when called anything else. Apparently this Jupiteran felt the same way. "You Plutonians have the brains of an Ursan rugworm, and your curling team couldn't win with ten extra rocks and a blindfolded referee."

Adequate Leader's antennae pointed angrily. "Go kiss a supernova, you little—"

"Hold it," I said quickly.

Lola texted, and words appeared in the air in front of me: *I'll call the Ambassador to calm them down. This is what he's here for, right?*

I gestured assent to Lola, keeping my attention on the screen. "There's no need for you to shoot at each other. Space is big enough for both of you to go on your way, and you won't have to cross paths. Where are you headed?"

"To the peace conference," they said simultaneously. The Jupiteran terminated the call and fired one last laser blast before zipping away.

"You should fix your camera," Adequate Leader told me. "It looks like it's snowing on your bridge." He disconnected.

I glared at the computer's control panel.

"Captain." Lola's aura shaded from pink to fuchsia. "Why don't I take over here for a while? You're going to wind up punching the computer."

Usually I was the one worrying about Lola's short temper, so if it was the other way around, something was wrong. I pulled myself to my feet, careful of the slippery deck. "I'll be in the view room."

I took a step, slipped on a patch of ice, and fell flat on my face. The computer giggled.

I stopped at the mess hall on my way upstairs. The detour took me down narrow corridors with sharp corners, past a series of dents in the wall. My ship had seen better days.

The mess hall was built for a half dozen crew members with varied eating habits. A pot of vegetable soup sat brewing next to a machine that condensed nutrients into crystals. The freezer contained some spices that were hot enough to be radioactive. I headed straight for the coffee maker, which was half empty and not even slightly warm.

Martian was sitting at the table while Pilar Villarreal, the ship's medical officer, pressed an ice pack to the back of his head.

"Hey, Janet." It's not very captain-like to let Martian call me that, but he's my younger brother, so I let it pass. "You missed a great snowball fight."

I poured the remains of the coffee into a cup and put it in the microwave. "Who won?"

"Nobody left standing." He took the ice pack from Pilar and returned it to the freezer. "But only because Lola wasn't there. Yesterday she clobbered all of us—even my snowball cannon was no help."

"No serious injuries this time," Pilar added. She had a motherly look, with graying brown hair and octagonal glasses. "I think the crew needs the outlet. Everyone's so frustrated since our last shore leave got canceled."

"Yeah." Martian was interrupted by the microwave making a shrill keening. He expertly jiggled the handle, and it stopped. "Hopefully Mom and Dad are still on Lyra II when we get there." Our parents were in the military, and Martian and I hadn't seen them in person since we joined GUPPEAS.

"I miss my family too," Pilar said. "I know the kids are enjoying college, but the last stop on Earth seems like ages ago."

College. If it hadn't been for that ridiculous arrest, I could have been in college, instead of here on a barely functional spaceship, dealing with the computer's attitude. "Martian, can you convince the computer that we don't need snow all over the ship?" I hadn't mastered the knack of giving orders instead of making requests. Months into this job, I still had trouble thinking of myself as a captain. "You're the only one the computer ever listens to."

"Sure." Martian exchanged a look with Pilar. What was that about? "You didn't get into another argument with it, did you?"

"That last one wasn't my fault. The computer—"

The microwave opened, and a mechanical arm handed me my coffee.

"Never mind. I'll be in the view room."

As the door closed behind me, I caught a few words from Pilar in a low voice: "We're going to have to do it."

Martian sounded troubled. "Yeah, you're right."

It had stopped snowing by the time I brought my coffee to the view room, which was a small space near the top of the ship, empty except for a bench facing a screen that covered one wall. I sat, realized too late that the bench was damp from the recent snowmelt, and jumped up again.

The screen showed our approach to Cygnus IV in the Pelican Nebula. For me, the view from space never got old. Twin suns burned red and yellow as the planet's cloud cover drew nearer. We were scheduled for a brief stop to drop off a passenger, and then my crew and I would head to Lyra for a much-needed shore leave. I should have been happy. Except I didn't want to let this passenger go.

I warmed my hands around the coffee cup and watched an endless array of stars grow dimmer.

The door slid open, and in walked the reason for my recent moodiness: Beau Dangere, the youngest ambassador in GUPPEAS, the peace organization that employed us both. A man of such good looks, warmth, intelligence, and charisma that it must have unbalanced the universe. To even it out, there had to be some unbelievably ugly, dumb, and mean man at the other end of the galaxy, or maybe in another timeline.

I didn't want to think about other timelines.

"Good morning." He stopped beside me, watching the planet with an innocent smile that sent my heart into overdrive. "I hear it's been a busy day already. Sorry I couldn't help, Captain."

"Not your fault. The other two ships were gone before Lola could get hold of you." I blew on the coffee. "You can call me Janet, you know."

"Are you sure that won't undermine your authority with your crew?"

In the distance, I could see other spaceships arriving. "You've been on my ship for three weeks. You can't seriously think I have any authority with my crew."

"Because you're young for a spaceship captain?"

That was an understatement. I was all of nineteen. "No, even if I wasn't, I'd still have a first officer with anger issues, a kleptomaniac pilot, a security chief who once restarted the war between Jupiter and Pluto, an engineer who's my actual brother, and a...whatever Zeeko's job is, he'd still be Zeeko."

"I'm pretty sure Dr. Villarreal respects you."

"Okay, that's one out of six." I took a gulp of coffee. "Looking forward to your new assignment?"

"Can't wait. Richena's ship should arrive around the same time as we do."

Richena. "That's great." The coffee burned the back of my throat.

There wasn't any socially acceptable way to say, *Your girlfriend, Richena, is a monster. You broke up with her, but you don't remember because she used time travel to rewrite history and take credit for my crew's heroism. She erased the whole timeline where you and I were in love. My crew and I are the only ones who remember, because of some weird time-particle effect on the ship that nobody except Martian understands. But every time I'm near you, I feel like a part of you still knows.*

"We have a little time before the peace conference starts," Beau said. "Richena and I should have a chance to catch up, maybe take in some curling."

"No, the sport," we said simultaneously.

He laughed. "It's amazing when you finish my sentences like that. Everyone else thinks I'm talking about hairdressing when I mention curling. Hard to believe we've only worked two missions together."

We'd known each other much longer, and much better, than he could imagine. We'd saved a planet together. I cleared my throat. "Some people click like that, I guess."

"Hope we get a chance to work together again." There was no hidden agenda behind his words, just his usual friendliness. He glanced at the bottom of the screen, where the ship's bow was visible. "The ship looks good now that they finally put the name on it."

"Yeah, I'm surprised it fit." Above the registration number, the hull now read *Cosmic Old York Nerthus Turkey.* It had taken ages for a committee to agree on that name. The ship had the awkward shape of a turkey, and occasionally made similar noises.

"They haven't decided on a name for Richena's ship. I think it looks like a dragon, or maybe a flying otter. She said maybe they should call it..."

He was still talking, but my mind was spinning too hard for me to focus. I wanted to tell him that he'd been tricked, everyone had been tricked, by Richena. Beau had been attracted by her bad-girl ways, but he'd found something better with me.

"Captain? Janet?"

"Sorry. Coffee hasn't kicked in yet. You were saying?"

"I hate to mention this, but something's missing out of my quarters."

Suppressing a groan, I pulled out my communication device and called the security chief. "Nlubglub, I need you to break into Frink's quarters and steal back an item that he took from Ambassador Dangere."

Beau looked embarrassed. "I wasn't accusing anyone."

"It was Frink. It always is." Nlubglub's voice squeaked with annoyance. "What's missing?"

"A diamond ring."

My heart punched me in the throat.

"Sorry about that." I kept my voice level. "Nlubglub, after you get it back—"

"Change the lock-code on the ambassador's guest quarters. Will do. Too bad Frink's so good at decoding them." Nlubglub disconnected.

I looked at Beau and grimaced. "I'll gently impress on Frink that it's bad manners to steal from a guest on our ship." Frink was a talented pilot, but he came from a planet where theft was less of a crime and more of a career choice. Anything that wasn't bolted down found its way into his quarters.

"Thanks." Beau smiled. His blue eyes were irresistible, and I had to suppress thoughts of our last kiss. As far as he knew, it had never happened. "About the peace conference. I've got a couple of concerns."

After this morning, I did too. "Like the fact that the participants are already shooting at each other?"

"No, that always happens. We'll probably have fistfights and tentacle-fights before the second day. But I noticed the Vegans are sending a contingent."

"Vegans?" I'd never had any issues with vegans. "Is there a problem with the menu?"

"Vegans, as in from Vega. And yes, there's a problem with the menu. They think humans are especially tasty."

"Ah."

"There's another thing." The double suns reflected off the clouds on the viewscreen, making his dark hair shimmer. "I may be wrong, but…does it seem like there's something sketchy about this peace conference?"

I made myself focus. "What do you mean?"

"The Cygnoids haven't always had the greatest relationship with other species. Now they suddenly have this plan to save the galaxy, but they won't tell us anything about it until the conference tomorrow."

"Could be an ego thing." With planetary leaders, that was inescapable. "But I agree, it feels a little off."

"Wish you were staying." There was a glint in his sapphire eyes that made me wonder: was it possible he remembered some hint of the other timeline? But all he said was, "I'd like another set of eyes on our hosts."

"Sorry, but GUPPEAS has been promising us shore leave on Lyra II, and we're not passing that up. Especially with my parents stationed there." I had so much to tell them, and it wasn't the same by message.

The door slid open. Zeeko stood in the entrance, wearing the perpetually surprised look of someone whose eyes resemble fried eggs.

"Captain, Lola punched the computer."

I returned to the bridge. The computer sported a fist-sized hole near the engineering station. Martian was tending to it. Not the actual repair yet; he was talking to the computer in a reassuring voice. "I'm sure Lola didn't mean it."

"Who cares what she meant?" The computer's metallic voice had more static than usual. "That hurt, and it was totally disrespectful. How would you like it if she smacked you?"

"She does, once in a while. I'm learning to dodge." He aimed a flashlight into the hole. "This won't hurt a bit." Martian loved machines, and machines loved him. The ship's computer went into frequent sulks when it wouldn't talk to anyone but him.

"It wasn't my fault," the computer whined. "All I did was deliver a message from Vertin Bogler at GUPPEAS headquarters."

"Bogler wasn't here to smack," Lola grumbled. Lola's aura was a dangerous crimson. "He wants us to stay for the peace conference. That means canceling shore leave."

I didn't punch anyone, but I may have thought about it.

"Let's take the shore leave anyway," Lola suggested. "The mission will probably get called off or changed before we're halfway through." This was all of our experience with the GUPPEAS bureaucracy.

"We could send holograms of ourselves to the conference," Martian suggested. "It won't take me long to design them."

The thought was tempting, but I was even worse at rule-breaking than at technology. "We'll do the mission. Maybe it will be a good one."

Pilar arrived to examine Lola's hand. "You're going to give yourself permanent damage if you keep doing this."

"What about the damage to me?" The computer sounded on the verge of tears, never mind that it wasn't technically possible.

"You'll be fine," Martian said soothingly. "Give me a millisecond."

"May as well get Frink and Nlubglub in here," I said, sending them a text. "We can get them filled in on the new assignment." I didn't bother calling Zeeko.

Nlubglub arrived moments later. Like the Jupiteran on the other ship, Nlubglub usually took the form of a large rubber ball with stubby legs. Nlubglub could imitate an infinite variety of shapes, but they always looked like they were made of bright purple rubber.

Frink slipped through the door a moment later, one arm half-hidden behind him. He stayed back instead of replacing Lola at the pilot's seat.

I eyed him suspiciously. "Frink, what do you have there?"

"Um, I don't know what you mean." Frink's voice dripped with innocence, as if we didn't all know better. He once stole an Olympic-sized swimming pool, then couldn't figure out where to hide it.

Lola's aura darkened again. "Let's see it." Her voice was enough to make clear she meant business. I've tried to cultivate a voice like that since becoming captain, unsuccessfully so far.

Frink pulled his hand out from behind his back. It was completely encased in a box labeled DO NOT TOUCH.

Martian laughed. "That's the lockbox I designed for Janet to safeguard her valuables."

Frink's orange eyes lit up as he turned to me. "You have

valuables?"

"No." On what GUPPEAS paid me, no chance. "That was a test run to make sure the box worked. Glad to see it did."

Pilar adjusted her glasses. Her hair was still dripping from the snowball fight. "Frink, there is treatment available for kleptomania."

"I know. I've stolen a few books about it." Frink glanced at Martian. "Could you get this thing off my hand so I can operate the controls?"

Martian remote-deactivated the lockbox with one hand and kept working on the computer with the other. Frink handed me the box and took his place at the pilot's seat, looking sheepish.

Zeeko wandered in, carrying an armload of light bulbs in various sizes. Since he didn't have a real job description, he was the unofficial cook, hairdresser, lizard-trainer, and a few other things.

I asked, "Do you want to know about the new assignment?"

"No," he said. "Do you?" He turned around and left, nearly crashing into Beau, who was on his way in.

"Ambassador, I was about to call you." Nlubglub pulled a box from inside the rubbery purple folds of their skin. Nlubglub didn't usually bother wearing a uniform, since it was easier to shape-shift without one. "I'll need you to identify which of these rings from Frink's quarters is the one that you're missing."

Beau's eyebrows jetted upward. "How many did he have?"

"Four," Nlubglub said.

"Seven," Frink said simultaneously. He clapped a hand to his mouth, then pulled it away. "Um, I meant four. It was totally four."

Nlubglub sprouted an extra eye from the back of their head to glare at Frink, and opened the box.

"That one." Beau picked up the ring. I tried not to be nosy, but the ring drew my eyes like a ship to a black hole. It was an elegant, heart-shaped stone. I hoped Richena would hate it.

Richena. The thought of him slipping it onto her finger was unbearable.

Nlubglub was still studying Frink. "Where did you get all these rings?"

"None of your business." Frink reached underneath his console where a handful of snow remained, and busied himself shaping it into a tiny snowman, using a thumbnail to give it leafy hair like his.

Nlubglub sprouted more eyes to look from one crew member to another. "Anybody missing one?"

Lola snorted. "Nobody here can afford diamonds. Nobody here can afford trapezoidal zirconia."

"They're mine," Frink said. "Give them back."

"I'll have to check with Zeeko first."

"Auto-canceling reservations for shore leave." The computer sounded a little too happy about it. "Including tickets to Galactic Curling Championship."

Lola smacked it with her uninjured hand.

"Entering orbit around Cygnus IV," Frink announced. The planet stretched out before us in gorgeous shades of pink and purple.

I hailed the office of the Counselor, the official leader of Cygnus IV, and was greeted by an assistant.

"This is Captain Janet Delane of the S.S. *Cosmic Turkey*. We're here for the peace conference, representing GUPPEAS."

The feathered assistant shuffled through some papers, looking harried. "Representing who?"

I had to look at the plaque on the wall to get the full name right. "The Galactic Universal Peacemongering Paradigm Emergent Action Spacefleet."

"Oh, them. What exactly is a paradigm?"

I was pretty sure I'd learned the word for a vocabulary test in high school, but that was one very long year ago. "It's hard to define, but it's a good thing. Can we get permission to land?"

The ship made a crunching noise, and plummeted toward the ground. "Frink, what's happening?" I yelled above the sound of engine gears grinding.

"Malfunction." Frink's voice rose with alarm. "Martian—"

"I'm on it." Martian ran toward the engine room.

We were plunging toward a space station below us. Frink worked the controls frantically, jerking the ship aside and missing the station by centimeters. My stomach tightened like a fist as we dropped. We passed through a cloud bank so thick that it gave the illusion we were standing still. But then we burst through into the sky above the planet, with the ground approaching much too fast.

"Found the problem." Martian's voice crackled over the intercom. "Keep us up here a minute longer." In the background, I heard the same noise the microwave had made earlier.

I wasn't sure we had a minute. Nlubglub contracted into a ball; they might survive the crash, but that didn't mean the rest of us would.

"Everyone strapped in?" I got a chorus of yeses in response. Except from Beau, who had no place to sit. I yanked him across my lap. "Hang on!"

Still dropping. We were about to die and I couldn't think of a witty exit line. Beau's arms tightened around me. Time seemed to slow down.

No, it was the ship slowing down. The ground was still approaching, but no longer at breakneck speed. Strain-neck speed, maybe. The fall eased to a stop, ten meters or so above the surface. Two avian creatures, who'd barely missed being hit by the ship, made a rude gesture as they flew away.

I looked up at Beau. He was blushing. I felt ridiculous with him on my lap, especially when I was so much smaller than he. "Sorry about that—"

Simultaneously, he said, "Thanks, quick thinking—"

The ship dropped the last ten meters and landed with a thud.

2

The List of Approved Hairstyles

I shifted underneath Beau so that I could breathe. "Everybody okay?"

Grudging yeses responded, one after another: Pilar, Frink, Lola. Over the intercom, Martian and Zeeko. Beau slowly pulled himself to his feet. Whose voice was missing?

"Nlubglub?"

"I think the fall scrambled my brains." Nlubglub was still in a ball. They slowly stretched back into their normal shape, growing eyes and then legs.

Pilar limped over to examine them. "Cellular strain. Keep shape-shifting to a minimum for the next few days."

Martian's voice came over the intercom again. "Not sure why, but the navigation got its coding crossed with the microwave in the mess hall. I'll get it fixed. Otherwise, we'll have to keep reheating coffee to get to our next destination."

"Great." I looked at the crumpled remains of my coffee cup on the floor. "Any idea where we are?"

Frink looked offended. "Right on target, of course. The dock outside the capital."

"Good work. I'll take a look outside and see what the damage is." If we could get the ramp down after that landing.

The ramp did go down, with a couple of extra shoves from the crew. Beau walked out with me. "Thanks for keeping me from getting crushed."

"My pleasure." As soon as that slipped out of my mouth, my cheeks warmed with embarrassment. "I mean, anytime."

We'd landed in a spaceport surrounded by gigantic trees. Some had been turned into buildings, with doors in their trunks, and walls built into the branches. The spaceport looked like the only clear spot around, and I sent a silent thanks for Frink's expert piloting. The pinkish-purple sky was visible in a narrow space between colorful leaves. There were other ships parked nearby: saucer-shaped, spherical, worm-shaped, and one that was made of living matter, constantly moving.

I stumbled on the ramp, and Beau caught my arm. "Thanks." I pulled away. "The gravity's a little lighter than I'm used to."

I glanced back at the ship, which was dented and scraped. The hull now appeared to read *Comic Oldy Turkey*. I'd have to check if Martian needed help from the Cygnoids for the repairs.

A red-feathered Cygnoid descended from the sky and landed on the dock. Despite wearing nothing but knee-length white pants, the Cygnoid looked solemn and formal—as near as I could read expressions on a human-sized bird with a giant beak like a toothy duck. "Greetings. I am Grebe, first assistant to the Counselor. He and him." Interplanetary protocol included exchanging pronouns to avoid awkward miscommunications.

"Honored to meet you. I'm Captain Janet Delane, she and her. This is Ambassador Beau Dangere, he and him."

Beau took his most ambassadorial tone. "We were sent by GUPPEAS on a mission of peace, and we look forward to meeting with the Counselor in order to—"

"Wait." Grebe's beak opened wide. "Did you say Janet Delane? I've heard of you." The formality gave way to excitement. "I love Pietro's column in the *Global Weekly*. The stories about your technology jinx are hilarious. Did you know he calls you Jam-it the Technology-Slayer?"

My throat tightened. "I'm aware." Light-years from home, and I still couldn't get away from my ex-boyfriend and his newspaper column.

"Can I take a selfie with you?" Grebe gushed. "The Counselor might want one too. He loved that story about how the coffee machine exploded when Pietro broke up with you."

"That's not exactly how it—"

"Beau!"

I knew that voice from my nightmares.

Richena Rossi pulled her floatcar to a stop next to my ship. She'd been driving with the top down, yet the knot of auburn hair on top of her head had stayed perfect, not a strand out of place. She climbed out of the car.

Richena was everything I wasn't. Tall and beautiful, dressed in a perfectly tailored silver uniform she'd designed herself, with unnecessary matching gloves. She was the captain of a large, sleek, dragon-shaped ship with a sizeable crew. She was a rising star in GUPPEAS, with an award named after her.

And she was Beau Dangere's girlfriend.

"Hi, Riche—"

Richena hurled herself into Beau's arms, and interrupted him with a forceful kiss.

Grebe watched, open-beaked. "That looks really unpleasant. Like some sort of cannibalism ritual."

"It's fine," I said, my mouth suddenly dry. "It's a custom among humans who know each other well."

Beau pried himself loose from Richena, grinning. "Missed you too."

"I was so worried when I saw the ship fall! I was afraid Janet's technology jinx would get you killed."

I faked a laugh, my nails digging into my palm. I was tired of hearing about my so-called technology jinx. It wasn't my fault that I always seemed to be nearby during minor computer glitches, anti-matter malfunctions, and one really unfortunate incident with a floatcar crashing into my hometown's city hall.

"Nice to see you again, Richena." I used my sweetest voice. "Hope you had a nice trip."

Richena kept her eyes on Beau. "We should get out of here."

"No," I said before I could stop myself.

Beau turned mildly curious eyes toward me. If only those eyes weren't such a perfect shade of royal blue. "Why not?"

I grabbed at the first plausible reason that came to mind. "I'm sure, as the ambassador, you'll want to meet our hosts."

"There's a formal dinner set for tonight." He glanced at Grebe. "Unless plans have changed?"

"The Counselor won't have time to meet anyone before then," Grebe said. "Can I get a selfie with each of you?"

Richena moved aside, stepping hard on my foot as she walked past. Grebe's selfie caught my wince at exactly the wrong moment.

When it was Richena's turn to pose, I walked toward her vehicle. "Snazzy floatcar." I raised my hand as if to touch it.

"Don't you dare." Richena kept her voice light, but I could hear the threat underneath. "If your technology jinx makes the car break down, Beau and I might be stuck together in some remote spot for hours and hours."

She had me there.

Beau looked enraptured, watching her. I spoke in an undertone. "You're going to pop the question, huh? Does she know?" They'd broken off a previous engagement right after my first mission, so maybe he was still undecided about it.

Beau looked at me. "What?"

"The ring. It's an engagement ring, right?"

He laughed. "Oh, no."

Relief filled me like a newly formed star bursting to life.

"That's the wedding ring. She proposed to me."

The star collapsed into a black hole.

Richena pulled off a glove to hold the camera, her engagement ring's dazzling sparkle outshone only by her smile.

On my way back to the ship, the gravity felt twice as heavy as it had with Beau around. I checked in with Martian, who was already elbows deep in repair work, and then I returned to my quarters.

My quarters were cramped, antiseptic-smelling, and a dreary gray, which the computer occasionally tried to liven up by putting motivational posters on the viewscreen. Today's poster showed a breathtaking view of a cliff over a purple ocean, and the words, "Take the first step."

"Not funny, computer," I muttered. I sat at my desk and got out my communication device, officially known as a beepity-beeper, which was short for Boron-Edged Electrum-Powered Integrated Technological Yadayada Bifurcated Electronic Eleventy-Purpose Existential Radio. The bureaucrats of GUPPEAS loved acronyms.

The beepity-beeper had multiple communication functions, including text, voice, video, and interpretive dance. No matter how many times I had Martian reprogram it, mine defaulted to letters appearing in the air and dissipating, making it hard to follow unless I read fast. Now, letters swirled around me as I dictated a message to Vertin Bogler and the rest of the GUPPEAS leadership, giving my opinion of them for canceling our shore leave. To my surprise, there was an emoji for "mildew-covered nest of Ursan rugworms." I ended by telling them I hoped they were eaten by a giant space squid that chewed very, very slowly.

I deleted it unsent.

Instead I recorded one for my parents. *Hi, bad news. Shore leave got canceled, so Martian and I won't get to see you right now. We're stuck in the Pelican Nebula. The Cygnoids are hosting a conference to announce a supposed peace plan for the galaxy. I have major doubts about that, and so does Ambassador Dangere.*

Lola thinks we should ignore the change in orders. Frink thinks we should pretend the message was garbled and we misunderstood it. Nlubglub claims to think we should do a surprise attack on Pluto, but I'm pretty sure they weren't serious. As for Zeeko, nobody knows what he thinks. Ever.

I glanced at my parents' last message to see if I'd forgotten anything. They'd said everything was fine on Lyra II, and that I shouldn't worry if I didn't hear from them for a while. They'd also asked if I was dating anyone. They always seemed to be asking me that, ever since my ex had landed a prestigious gig writing for an interplanetary news service.

No, I'm definitely not seeing anyone right now. Much too busy being a spaceship captain.

I hit Send and stared moodily at cliffs over a purple ocean.

The welcome banquet was a formal affair, meaning I wore a ten-colored monstrosity of a uniform instead of the usual eight-colored one. I tried to put aside my misgivings. The Cygnoids had invited species from every corner of the quadrant, all of whom attended in the interest of promoting peace. It seemed a good sign that the Cygnoid leader went by the modest title of Counselor. After recent encounters with Exalted Leader (Pluto), Her Supreme Superiority (Venus), and Dude Who Signs the Paychecks So You'd Better Salute (Gemini XII), this suggested we were dealing with someone a little more down-to-Earth. Down-to-Cygnus-IV. Whatever.

The Great Hall wasn't built inside a tree, but rather around one the size of a city block. Flowering branches made up the walls and ceiling of the dining room, and the floor was a mosaic of colored glass. The air was filled with rich spices and the smell of fresh bread as my crew and I were ushered to our table. Other guests shuffled, flapped, and oozed in: floppy-faced Plutonian reptiles, shape-shifting Jupiterans, giant slugs from Kappa Leporis, flying insects from Antares, glowing Venusians, furry mammals from Polaris. A series of tanks contained water-breathing attendees, and three stoppered bottles held gaseous creatures. A vast chattering crowd surrounded me, one smallish primate from Earth.

I tensed as Beau and Richena entered. Beau looked dashing in a tuxedo, and Richena had skipped the dress uniform in favor of a slinky black dress and crystal necklace. My eyes automatically went to her hand, wondering how much time before a wedding ring joined the elegant engagement ring.

My crew settled into chairs at one of the long tables. Other attendees in GUPPEAS uniforms joined the crowd, presumably members of Richena's crew. Among them I recognized Skeeder Boredan, the only Plutonian in GUPPEAS, and the guilty party behind our current uniform design. He'd spent one mission stowed away aboard the *Turkey*. Tonight he was wearing a robe stitched together from different-colored socks, with a matching hat atop his antennae. A smile crossed his gray-green face when he saw me.

As Beau and Richena reached the table, something caught Beau's attention nearby. Lowering his voice, he asked, "Does she look familiar?"

Richena looked over at the next table. "Should she?"

I furtively checked out the woman he'd indicated. She appeared humanoid, with dark glasses and an elaborate braided hairdo. I racked my brain, replaying our recent missions. She didn't look familiar, but she *felt* familiar, if that made any sense.

I couldn't tell for sure with the dark glasses, but I thought she winked at me.

"Hey!" Richena had Frink by the wrist. "Hands off my purse."

"Sorry." Frink strolled back to his seat, as if being caught in petty larceny was the most normal thing in the universe.

I took advantage of the distraction to move to the seat next to Beau, with Richena on his other side. A moment later, Richena noticed and her face smoldered, but whatever she said was lost in the applause as the Counselor rose. Richena casually reached past Beau for the bread and tipped over a glass, splashing bright red juice onto my uniform. I grabbed a napkin and tried to sop up the mess, although with so many colors in the uniform, one more didn't make much difference. I ignored Richena's faux apology for the "accident," keeping my eyes on the Counselor.

He was an older Cygnoid, as near as I could tell, with silver-gray feathers. As was the Cygnoid custom, he wore loose pants and no shirt. Unlike the others, the Counselor had a sheer white cape that seemed to flutter by itself.

"Welcome, honored guests. While we come from many worlds and traditions, one custom that is nearly universal is sharing food as a gesture of friendship. Erm, except on Vega, where the Vegans tend to eat their dinner guests. They'll be joining us after the banquet. We've brought a variety of delicacies from all of your worlds. Everyone, please enjoy."

"Hang on," Nlubglub said. "He can't say it's universal. Sharing food is not a Jupiteran custom."

"Well, sure," Pilar said, "but you don't eat. You're more mineral than animal."

"Exactly," Nlubglub said. "On Jupiter, a gesture of friendship would be a game of billiards."

Lola rolled her eyes. "Last time you were in a friendly billiard game, you started a riot."

"That was the Plutonians' fault. They totally cheated—"

Skeeder's antennae snapped upward. "Did not."

"Excuse me," Beau said firmly, "we're at a peace conference."

"And, Frink," I added, "put back that wallet you lifted." I hadn't seen it happen, but with Frink it was a pretty fair bet.

"Okay, but I get to keep the earrings, right?"

"No."

A twelve-tentacled server laid down a tray in front of me, filled with my favorite foods: Saturnian fruits, a savory Ursan stew, and a hot pepper that spontaneously combusted over the vegetables. The bread tasted like lilacs. Most importantly, there were chocolate chip cookies.

At the next table, the woman with the braids devoured a hot fudge sundae with a look of ecstasy. A suspicion began to form in my mind.

There was a young man sitting next to her, in nondescript gray clothes. His food sat untouched as he looked around in cheerful curiosity. He caught my eye, smiled, and quickly looked away.

After the plates were cleared off, I noticed a collection of teeth walking in. They belonged to aliens the size of buffalo, with armored skin like gray scaly turtles. But I mostly saw their teeth, which were gigantic and impossibly numerous and very, very sharp.

I nudged Beau. "Are those who I think they are?"

"Vegans."

The Counselor once again took center stage. "My friends, for too long our worlds have fought over every possible issue. Political systems. Distribution of resources. Table tennis scores. One solar system was nearly annihilated because the Plutonians believe there are two genders and Jupiterans believe there are forty-six."

"Forty-seven," the woman at the next table called with a smile.

"Two!" A furious Plutonian sprang to his feet.

"Is this worth fighting a war over?" The Counselor's voice was soothing and rational. "Especially when you're both wrong. There are five."

Nlubglub's face flattened in surprise. "What?"

The Plutonian delegates were outraged, and Skeeder as well. "You're wrong about everything, just like the Jupiterans are wrong about everything. And they have no fashion sense. And they accused us of cheating at billiards."

Nlubglub wasn't going to let that pass. "You cheat at billiards, and you have the worst curling team in the galaxy."

"Your mother was a one-eyed Saturnian blobfish—"

"You lose every war and you have the brains of a Neptunian swamp bug—"

"Hold it!"

Everyone looked around to see who had spoken. Unfortunately, it was me.

I took a deep breath. "You're at a peace conference. You must have some reason to think peace is a good thing. Our Cygnoid friends are trying to offer a solution. That's what you came here for, so don't laser yourself in the foot before finding out what they have to say. You can always go back to having these arguments later, right?"

Nlubglub sat back down. After a moment, Skeeder and the other

Plutonians did too. The man at the next table gave me a thumbs-up. When I took my seat, Beau put a hand on my shoulder. "That was impressive, Captain."

"Thanks." My shoulder tingled after he took his hand away.

The Counselor beamed at me. "Thank you, Captain Delane. This is a perfect example of what we're up against: age-old rivalries that keep getting worse, each generation adding new offenses to avenge. Left to your own devices, the hostilities are going to continue until somebody accidentally destroys the universe. You can see there's only one solution."

The Counselor looked around, smiling, waiting for applause. There were puzzled looks instead. Beau asked, "What solution is that, exactly?"

"Putting us in charge."

"*Us*, as in...Cygnoids?"

"Of course." The Counselor's fatherly tone never faltered. "We have a far superior culture to any of your planets, no offense. We can calculate the best use of all your planets' resources and eliminate any sporting events that could lead to excessive conflict."

"What?" Voices piped up from different parts of the room.

"And there are other improvements you need to make," the Counselor continued, not a single feather ruffled. "Jupiterans, you haven't made a good holofilm in fifty of your years. Plutonians, stop calling yours a real planet. You're not fooling anyone. And, Earthlings, where do I start?"

Outraged attendees stormed toward the podium, shoving and cursing. Nlubglub and Skeeder were marching side by side. They leapt to the front of the crowd—only to crash against a force field surrounding the podium.

The Counselor gave a dismissive wave at the would-be invaders. "We're sending each of you a list of the modifications your people will make."

A list scrolled in front of me as if I were looking at a viewscreen. *Modifications for Earth:*

1. *Move all the continents back together into a single continent.*
2. *Add perches on all building roofs for avian visitors.*
3. *Ban kissing, as it is unhygienic and resembles cannibalism.*
4. *Have more humor at funerals...*

All around me, people were sputtering with rage over the demands. Richena shrieked when she saw the list of approved hair-styles. "Mullets?"

The Counselor was unmoved. "We'll make the rules, you'll all follow them, and we won't ever have to use the Civilizer."

A screen lit up above the Counselor, displaying a complex machine with a constantly changing light display across its surface. It looked like a clock running backward while having the time reset for Daylight Saving during time travel. There was a missile-like extension pointed outward.

"The Civilizer is capable of inflicting unthinkable agony on you," the Counselor continued pleasantly. "But we're certain you'll be reasonable. Let us know when you agree to our list of demands. Enjoy the dessert buffet." He exited through a door behind the podium, into the trunk of the tree, and the force field shimmered and disappeared.

Some of the crowd rushed forward and pounded on the door. Others headed for the dessert buffet. I hung back with my crew. "Any idea what that weapon was?"

"No way to know without examining it up close," Martian said. "For all we know, it could be an empty cylinder and this is all a giant bluff."

"Possibly," Nlubglub said. "But that doesn't seem like a good thing to take a chance on."

Lola's aura was a deep orange. "We should go back to the ship and figure out our next move."

Zeeko looked confused. "What about dessert?"

3

Long Walks on the Beach

Back at the ship, we regrouped and tried to make sense of what had happened. Pilar said, "We need to contact GUPPEAS and let them know about this so-called peace plan."

"Yeah." Lola's aura crackled with irritation. "They'll set up a committee to study it."

"I think you have to request a committee by filling out a form in triplicate," Zeeko said helpfully.

"We need to get rid of this Civilizer, whatever it is." Nlubglub drummed a half dozen tentacles on the table. "Otherwise they'll cancel curling, and completely mess up Jupiteran cinema."

"And basically make all species besides Cygnoids into prisoners," Frink added. A dozen pieces of silverware fell out of his sleeve.

"But we don't know what this weapon is." Martian's round face was tight-lipped with worry.

"Does it matter?" Lola gave me an appraising look. "We get the captain to touch it, and the machine will fall apart, right?"

I blinked. "Wait, what?"

"Not necessarily," Pilar said. "What if it's some sort of bio-weapon? I'm pretty sure her technology jinx only works on mechanical stuff."

"You know that whole 'technology jinx' thing is totally exaggerated." Bad enough I had to read about it in Pietro's column, but now I had to hear it from my crew too? "All of those incidents had logical

29

explanations. Well, some of them did, anyway."

They all looked at me, then went back to strategizing. "The technology jinx could be Plan A, but we need a Plan B," Martian said.

"We can have a whole alphabet of plans, but it's not going to matter unless we know where to find it," Nlubglub pointed out. "They're not going to have it anywhere accessible."

"What are our options?" I looked from one face to another. "Do we have any?"

"Find a way to spy on them," Martian suggested. "You can't build a powerful weapon without a lot of resources, and you have to guard and maintain it afterward. It should be possible to narrow down the location."

"There's always diplomacy," Pilar said. "Convince them their plan is...how to put this...completely bananas."

I seized on that. "Maybe Beau Dangere can talk sense into them. He's very persuasive. I should call him."

Martian and Pilar exchanged a look, like they had earlier in the kitchen. What was that about?

Frink shook his head, his leafy green hair flapping. "The ambassador can try, but I don't think the Cygnoids will listen to reason."

"Let me guess." Lola side-eyed Frink. "Your solution is stealing the weapon."

Frink looked like he wanted to deny it, but he had a pile of stolen silverware in front of him. "Depending on the value of the parts, we can pay for fuelstone for a long time." He started building a small tower out of the silverware, fitting knives and forks together.

"I know how to find it." Nlubglub's face perked up. "We tell them the Plutonians broke one of their stupid rules, and then they'll use the weapon on the Plutonians."

"Nlubglub." I tried not to yank my hair out. "What part of *peace organization* do you not understand?"

"They're Plutonians. They've started more wars than any other species. They tried to ban chocolate, and they're always misgendering me. Do I even look like a *him*?"

"Of course not," I assured them, "but at least the Plutonians aren't trying to ban Jupiteran cinema, like our hosts here."

"Oh. Right." Nlubglub scrunched their rubbery purple face in thought. "What if we convince the Cygnoids that we have a weapon that's more powerful than theirs?"

All eyes turned to Martian. "A fake weapon? I've never even invented a real one. You wouldn't let me."

"No one would believe we had a weapon," Lola pointed out. "Peace organizations don't run around with them."

"The Cygnoids do, and they claim it's for peace," Zeeko said. I'd almost forgotten he was there. He nodded at Frink's silverware tower. "That's very artistic. Did you ever consider a career in art theft?"

"I'm starting to like the framing-the-Plutonians idea," Lola said. The pinkish-red of her aura was simultaneously pleased and dangerous.

"We are not framing the Plutonians." How in the universe had I wound up with this job? Why couldn't I have gone to college or kept working in the edible-air factory? "We are going to find this Cygnoid weapon, if it's real, and figure out how to deactivate it."

"That was your plan coming in," Lola said. "Why did you bother asking for options?"

"I was hoping someone had a better idea."

"Message incoming from GUPPEAS." How did the computer's voice sound so pleased with itself?

"Play the message," Lola said. "Or don't. Whatever."

Vertin Bogler's face appeared on the screen. "Change of plans. You're rerouting to Vega to recruit the Vegans into joining GUPPEAS. There are a number of important protocols that need explaining, so pay close attention." He glanced at his notes. "First of all, don't arrive near mealtime."

I thought of the toothy Vegans at the banquet and shuddered.

Pilar switched off the recording. "What a shame the message didn't get through."

"Yeah." Martian gave an exaggerated shrug. "I've been having real problems with the communications equipment."

Lola grabbed Frink's silverware and threw a fork at the wall, then a knife. "I'm pretty sure it said to take that shore leave they promised us earlier on Lyra II."

"Sounded like Rigel V to me," Frink said.

"We need to figure out how to get rid of this weapon, or shore leave will be the least of our problems," I said. "So as far as I'm concerned, we didn't hear any message."

Zeeko scratched his giant cone-shaped ears, bewildered. "My hearing's pretty good. We could play it back again."

The entire crew glared at him with varying degrees of annoyance. "No."

The next morning started out ordinary. I walked onto the bridge, where Lola had Frink pinned against the wall, yelling in his face. "Give it back! It's my favorite knife!"

"I can explain—"

Nlubglub walked in, coolly appraised the situation, and grew a dozen fast-moving tentacles to search Frink, finding a pearl-handled knife and a diamond ring. Lola snatched the knife away.

"Wait." I took a close look at the ring. "This looks like the one Beau had."

Nlubglub sprouted an extra eye to examine it. "It's the same ring. How'd you manage to steal it again already?"

Frink wiggled free of Lola and took a step away, looking uncertainly at the knife. "It fell out of his pocket during the crash, and rolled over to me. You can't expect me to leave it lying there when it was practically a gift."

"It's not yours." I pocketed the ring. "I'll give it back to him."

"Okay, but if he drops it again—"

"Tell him."

"And leave my knives alone." Lola's voice was sharper than the blade.

"How are you allowed to have weapons?" Frink kept his distance. "We're a peace organization."

"They're not weapons. They're decorative." She waved the knife in front of Frink. "And if you touch them again, I'll decorate you."

"Shut up, all of you! You sound like a bunch of babbling Neptunian croakbirds."

All eyes turned to me.

I wanted to smack myself. "Sorry. I don't know what came over me there." Which might not sound captain-like either, but I wasn't raised to be rude.

"Captain," Nlubglub said gently, "maybe you could use some coffee."

I dragged myself to the mess hall and brewed a pot of coffee, avoiding the microwave, which now had several new wires connecting it to a pipe in the wall.

I scrolled Pietro's column in the *Galactic Times*. He'd already gotten pictures of our crash landing. *"Has Jam-it's technology jinx finally gone too far? The* Turkey *looks like Thanksgiving leftovers."* An item at the end of the column bragged that he would be the wardrobe consultant for the upcoming wedding of a soon-to-be-named spaceship captain and an ambassador. He had all kinds of opinions about cummerbunds.

I was busy being a spaceship captain, I reminded myself, and that meant focusing on the mission. We'd come expecting peace, and now we were dealing with the threat of conquest. Beau had been right about the Cygnoids. How was he so wrong about Richena?

How was I back on Beau?

Pilar sat down next to me, looking over the top of her glasses. "Captain, you're worrying us. Breakups happen. You have a ship to run." She slid a chocolate cupcake next to my coffee.

"I know, but it's not an ordinary breakup." And Beau wasn't an ordinary guy. "Maybe if I could go back in time again, I could fix—"

"Janet." Martian sat down across from me. "You and time-travel technology don't mix."

"Time travel?" That was Lola, coming up behind me. "You and any technology don't mix. You should come with a warning sign. One that's not electronic."

Nlubglub stretched so their rubbery face could be seen above the other crew members. "The important thing is, you can't let your personal life mess up your work life. You have responsibilities. And take it from someone who's been around a century or three longer than you have: you'll get over him. There are plenty of other stars in the galaxy."

"I don't want other stars," I grumbled. "And what are all of you doing in here? Shouldn't someone be on duty?"

"Zeeko's on duty." Frink squeezed into the last remaining place at the table. "And this is an intervention."

I wasn't sure which piece of information was more alarming. Zeeko was not exactly known for rational thought. On the other hand, this was a *what?* "Intervention?"

Everyone seemed to be looking at everyone else, nobody wanting to start. Finally Pilar cleared her throat. "You tried to win an argument with the computer last week when it wanted to play background music. You got the computer so upset that it blasted Neptunian opera half the night."

"The computer needs an intervention, not me." The drum solos had been bad enough, but the calliope music every time something malfunctioned was taking it too far.

"You said its mother was a defective printer," Martian said. "How is that not going to hurt the computer's feelings?"

"Computers don't have mothers. And they don't have feelings."

"You're definitely wrong on that last part," Martian said. "It was practically crying on my shoulder."

"And another thing." Lola's aura was straying into angry magenta territory. "I got a message from Vertin Bogler at GUPPEAS, saying you told him the crew was debating whether to ignore the new assignment or creatively misinterpret it."

"What? I haven't talked to him."

Lola showed me the message on her beepity-beeper. It was the one I'd meant to send to my parents. I stared at it, eyes watering with embarrassment. The higher-ups at GUPPEAS would... Well, they would probably set up a committee to decide what to do, and eventually forget about it. That was how they handled most problems.

"Obviously we do those things, but we don't tell GUPPEAS about it." Nlubglub's squeaky voice rose. "It's like you don't care anymore about acting like a real captain."

"Did I ever?"

All their voices at once: "Yes!"

"Fortunately, I have the solution." Frink pulled up a page on his beepity-beeper. "Have you seen this new dating site, LuckyStar?"

I checked out the page. It showed the smiling faces of Fibby and Queelchu, the Plutonian/Jupiteran couple who had founded the company. Both of them looked blissfully happy in a way I'd never seen when I'd met them in person. They were surprisingly cute, now that they were together.

A series of notifications popped up. Frink scrolled down, grinning. "More matches for me. They've got someone for every taste: men, women, non-binaries. Non-trinaries."

"I'm only into men." Only into one man, and he wasn't here.

"Suit yourself. But you should check out the quadri-gendered Rigelians. They're really different."

I wanted to scream at everyone to go away. But these were my crewmates, my friends, and it wasn't their fault I was miserable. They were trying to help.

I looked from one face to another. "I appreciate what you're trying to do. But I need to wallow in my misery for a while. This is how I get over things." I hoped.

Frink sent the page to my beepity-beeper. "I took the liberty of creating a profile for you."

"You did?" I looked over the profile. The accompanying photo wasn't terrible, so Zeeko must have done my hair that day. More importantly, it was taken during the brief period when GUPPEAS uniforms were lavender, instead of the current motley horrors.

I read what Frink had written for me:

Hi, I'm Janet Delane (she/her) from Earth. At 19, I'm the youngest spaceship captain in GUPPEAS. My crew is awesome, but I'm looking for that special someone. My hobbies are low-tech: long walks on the beach, science fiction books, quality chocolate, and curling (no, the sport). I can't dance but will fake it enthusiastically. No psycho exes, please—my awesome crew has been through enough.

Did I like long walks on the beach? Had I ever been on one? The beaches around my hometown had been invaded by escaped Plutonian chomperfish, so no one went near them.

And how did Frink know I didn't dance? Oh yeah, *that* video, which everyone had seen thanks to my own psycho ex, Pietro.

"It can't hurt," Frink said.

I had no idea how wrong he was.

Later in my quarters, I double-checked that my door was locked and then scrolled through the LuckyStar site.

I made a few edits on the profile, cutting out the references to dancing and the awesomeness of my crew. I left in the long walks on the beach, since everyone else's profile seemed to have that one. Maybe it was required. And I left in the "no psycho exes" part, thinking of how Richena had done everything to sabotage Beau and me. Except, of course, she was no longer his ex.

I swiped from one picture to the next, skipping the ones that posed with large firearms or their first three wives.

"Looking for a homebody to settle down and have dozens of kids." Swipe left.

"Looking for companion on dangerous mission in the Lilliput galaxy." Swipe left.

"Looking for meaningless relationship, send picture from neck down, please." Swipe left faster.

"Looking for a woman with intelligence, warmth, and a sense of humor. A plus if her hobby is curling." Swipe—wait, that picture looked familiar. It was the guy who'd given me the thumbs-up at the banquet. He was nice looking and close to my age, his profile sounded okay, and we had the same hobby. His name was Randy Miv.

I swiped right.

A few minutes later, he sent a message. The letters poured out of my beepity-beeper, as if he was typing at superhuman speed: *I saw you at the banquet, and your speech was amazing. You're with GUPPEAS? That's the peace organization, right?*

Yes, and thanks. What brought you to the conference?

I'm from Cassiopeia VII, he answered. This meant nothing to me. While I was still trying to formulate a question that sounded halfway intelligent, he sent another message. *There's an interplanetary comedy troupe performing tomorrow night. I have no idea if they're any good or not. Take a chance with me?*

4

Two to the Power of Splat

Randy met me at the comedy show, looking attractively informal in a button-down shirt and khakis. I wore a red dress, glad to be out of uniform for a change. I'd had Zeeko do my hair for an extra dose of confidence. The club was small and dimly lit, at the top of a very tall tree, with stars visible through the leafy ceiling. It had a solid floor, though I had to be careful not to let my heels catch on the uneven wood.

The Plutonian comic was so bad, it made my teeth hurt. Humor varies from one planet to the next, but there are only so many ways you can recycle the joke about how Jupiterans dance like *this*, and Plutonians dance like *that*.

"What's the deal with Jupiterans? They don't eat or drink, most of them are centuries old, and how are you supposed to know if you're using the right pronoun?"

"Ask, dummy!" a heckler yelled.

"And that whole shape-shifting thing. If you could look like any-thing, would you pick a giant rubber ball with legs?"

"Do Earthlings next," someone else called—and this one's voice was familiar. I looked around and spotted a Venusian's purple aura. He was so giddy with laughter that I could hardly make out his face in the incandescent violet glow, but I recognized my ex-boyfriend Pietro.

"Yeah, what about those Earthlings? Here's how they dance." The comic did a poor rendition of the Ditzy Space Owl, a dance that no one had done in the last two years. I was probably the last one who'd ever tried it. "And, Venusians, what's with those auras? Did you know they don't have auras on their home planet because it's too hot?"

"Everyone knows that," Randy whispered. He was cute when he wrinkled his nose. "Do you want to skip the rest of the show? Go dancing, maybe?"

I was not ready to have Randy see me dance. "Let's stay. Maybe the next act will be better."

The comic was just getting started. "And what's going on over on Cassiopeia VII? But we know how they dance over there." He did a stiff-armed lurch around the stage.

"I have no idea what that's supposed to be," Randy said.

"Seriously, what's going on over there?" the comic droned on. "Nobody's been able to communicate with them in weeks. Is there a new world order, or are they ghosting us?"

"Is that true?" I asked. "No communication with Cassiopeia VII?" I'd never been to his planet and knew almost nothing about that system.

"Yeah. Not since the rebellion started." He avoided my eyes.

"You must be worried about your family."

"They're not on Cassiopeia."

The comic added, "Now the Galactic Military Federation is talking about going over there to check it out. Will they be met by an army of killer droids, or the galaxy's largest pile of scrap metal?"

Randy looked as surprised as I was. "The Galactic Military? When did this happen?"

My mind was racing. My parents were in the military, and they had mentioned being sent on a new mission. Probably a coincidence. They could be going anywhere. But I was too distracted to notice the rest of the comic's set.

At intermission, I ordered two coffees. I was tempted to interrogate Randy about his planet, but he seemed reluctant to talk about it. And I didn't know if my parents were headed there. My needless worrying shouldn't be his problem. I sent off a quick text to my parents.

When I looked up, Pietro slid into the seat next to me, his purple aura sparkling. "Hi, Janet, funny how we keep running into each other. Sure you're not following me?" Pietro gave an awkward laugh.

"I'm here on a date." I turned to Randy, on the other side of me. "Randy, this is Pietro, my ex. I don't know what he's doing here."

"You may have seen my column in the *Galactic Times*," Pietro said, reaching across me to shake hands. "It's called *Primarily Pietro*."

"Can't say that I have." Randy kept his voice nicely bland.

Pietro's aura faded a little. "How did you two meet?"

"I saw Janet on LuckyStar. It's amazing how many things we matched on. We like the same curling teams."

"A dating app? That's so…last week." Pietro, who obsessively researched next week's fashions, considered this the ultimate insult.

"That's the beauty of it," I said. "I can find someone who shares my total lack of interest in whether something is *so last week*."

The coffees arrived. Randy gave me a surprised look. "Oh. I don't drink coffee."

No coffee? Maybe we were less compatible than I thought. "What would you like?"

"Nothing right now, thanks."

I didn't know what to say next. Pietro, however, didn't have that problem. "I came here to write a column about the peace conference, since it has luminaries like Richena Rossi here representing GUPPEAS." I was also here representing GUPPEAS, but wasn't going to get baited into pointing that out. "Weird how it turned out, huh?"

"'Weird' would be one word for it," Randy said mildly. "So would 'catastrophic,' 'horrifying,' and a number of Cassiopeian words I probably shouldn't use in public."

Pietro leaned toward me, grinning. "What do you think Richena's plan will be? Full-frontal assault?"

"You know GUPPEAS is a peace organization, right?" Why did I have to keep explaining this to people? "The P stands for Peace-mongering."

"Right. So is Richena going to send in her ambassador fiancé to negotiate?"

Sitting in between my ex-boyfriend and possibly-next boyfriend, I felt a pang of longing for a man who'd never been my boyfriend in this timeline. "That would be a smart thing to do." I took a gulp of coffee. "Send in an experienced diplomat who can help all sides find common ground."

Pietro snorted. "If it's the smart thing, then GUPPEAS will do the exact opposite."

Which was accurate, but I didn't care to have Pietro bad-mouthing my organization. "We can't all be geniuses like you."

Intermission over, the next comic was a Venusian man with a sparkling blue aura. "Venusians! Let's face it, we're the worst. We all have, like, twenty-three names, and we have a fit if anybody gets them in the wrong order." That was a slight exaggeration: my first officer had seven names, only four of which fit on her official ID, and she let me call her Lola because she said nobody pronounced Lolagnya right.

The comic continued, "But the worst thing? Venusian men. We all think we're brilliant. We wake up with a cool idea for how to reorganize society, and spend the rest of the night congratulating ourselves on how we're going to win the GUPPEAS Peace Prize and have rock musicals written about us. We text all our friends about it. Then we wake up to a dozen messages pointing out that somebody else already thought of the same thing, and it turned into a disaster that almost got the entire planet eaten by a giant space squid."

I gave Pietro a thoughtful look. "That sounds like the time you thought you'd invented—"

"No, it doesn't." His aura dialed back down to lavender.

The comedian drowned out any response I might have made. "And what's the deal with Mercurians? No one ever understands what they're talking about. You ask them what's the temperature outside, and they'll tell you two to the power of splat equals a flying mushroom."

Pietro snickered. "That does sound like a typical conversation with Zeeko."

Bad enough he'd invited himself to our table, and now he was insulting my crew. "Pietro, did you not hear me say that I'm here on a date? Could you give us a little space?"

Pietro mumbled an apology and moved away.

The next couple of acts were equally forgettable. Then, with a sinister rattling of teeth, a Vegan comic strode onto the stage and grabbed the microphone. "The first person who doesn't laugh gets to be a snack."

Randy and I fake-laughed all the way to the elevator as we fled.

"I'm sorry the show wasn't more enjoyable," he said as we rode the elevator down. "I was expecting better than tired ethnic clichés."

"Not your fault. We'll find something better next time. And I'm sorry about my ex showing up—I had no idea he would be here." My mind was aflutter with the do-we-kiss-or-don't-we dilemma that makes first dates so terrifying. I should have read up more on his planet's customs. Did he look pleased when I'd hinted there could be a next time?

We stepped off the elevator on the ground floor, then stood there for an awkward moment, our separate floatcars waiting for us. Finally he said, "Good night," and started to move his face toward mine.

A cone-eared Mercurian woman came racing between us, almost knocking me over. I registered that she had on sunglasses like the ones on the human woman at the banquet.

Two Cygnoids in security uniforms ran between us, chasing after her. She disappeared into the elevator, and the doors closed a moment before the Cygnoids reached it.

Randy and I watched with curiosity as the guards pulled off a wall panel next to the elevator and yanked the wires out of their sockets. A minute later, the elevator returned, and a bright yellow Jupiteran walked out.

"Where's the Mercurian?" the Cygnoids demanded.

"Was that the person with the huge ears? Got off at the eighth floor." The Cygnoids flew up through the branches.

I looked back at the elevator and asked Randy, "Do you smell smoke?"

"No."

I didn't see any smoke. Maybe I'd imagined it.

The Cygnoids flew back down. "Are you sure it was the eighth floor?"

"Not totally," the Jupiteran said.

The mood was definitely broken. "Well...good night." Randy headed toward his floatcar.

The Jupiteran sauntered past, giving me a wink. I'd seen eyes that shade of aqua before.

The next morning found me sitting in the mess hall with my first cup of coffee, scrolling port logs for the names of ships docked nearby. The aqua-eyed Jupiteran had left me curious. I found the listing I was looking for, and sent a text: *Can we talk? I'll meet you at the chocolate shop.*

Minutes later, I got an audio message from an unfamiliar name, and played it back. The voice was musical, pinging from low notes to high ones like a piano.

We have been trying to reach you about the extended warranty for your spaceship. You have a limited time to respond—

I hit Delete so hard my finger stung. Was there anywhere in the universe to get away from those scam calls?

Another message popped up. My throat tightened, thinking it might be my parents, but it was from Beau. *Weirdest thing, the ring's disappeared again. Any chance your sticky-fingered pilot "found" it again? We're thinking about moving up the wedding date, since the Counselor's got this crazy idea about choosing people's mates for them.*

The ring. I'd forgotten to return it to him.

And he hadn't noticed until now?

I headed back to my quarters to get it. When I opened the door, Frink was standing over my desk with the ring and a pile of my belongings in front of him: an anti-radiation umbrella, a box of chocolates, and a book I'd bought and hadn't read yet: *U, Robot,* by Isaac Androidov. Not noticing my entrance, Frink reached for my alarm clock, but was distracted by a notification sounding on his beepity-beeper, and he sat down to scroll.

I looked over his shoulder. He was reading through message after message on LuckyStar.

A woman from Scorpio VI wrote, *I can't believe they fired you from your job, when you were already having trouble making rent. Especially when they know you have Klobberz Disease! I'm sending 500 credits, hope this helps. Don't worry, once you move here with me, medical care is free, like it is on every civilized world.* There were similar messages from an Orion man and a non-binary Venusian.

What were they talking about? No one got fired from GUPPEAS—not even Frink was that lucky—and there wasn't any rent on a spaceship. And Pilar had just given him a physical. Other than a couple of bruises from that argument with Lola, he was in perfect health.

Frink looked up and saw me. He nearly dropped the beepity-beeper. "It's not what you think."

"Which part?" Exasperation was raising my blood pressure. "You burglarizing my quarters again, or—"

"You finally got some new books. I've read that one about curling at least three times."

"—or the fact that you're using the dating site to run scams on people?"

"No. Yes. But it's not for me." Frink clicked over to another page. "It's for Xerxzez."

"Xerxzez?"

Frink pulled up a profile of a quadri-gendered Rigelian. *Hi, I'm Xerxzez (they/them). I run an interplanetary curio shop, buying and selling everything from Orion jewelry to Betelgeuse booze and antique curling stones. It makes my hearts pound when I discover an obscure video game from a planet in a remote quadrant. Other things that make my hearts pound: dinner by candlelight, slow dancing, Ursan art, long walks on the beach, and six-fisted boxing.*

"We've been in an online relationship for a few months now. We were finally going to meet in person at our last stopover on Kappa

Leporis, but they messaged me that their business was really hurting for money, and they couldn't afford to travel. I'm helping them get their business back on its feet." Frink's orange eyes shone with adoration.

"It's still not okay to scam all those other people. You need to return the money."

"I can't. I already sent it to Xerxzez."

"Frink, you need to repay that money, and not by stealing it from someone else. Otherwise I'll have to tell Xerxzez that you're a crook who's only trying to take advantage of them."

Frink blanched. "But that's not true. I mean, it's true about me being a crook. But I really like Xerxzez. I think they're the one for me."

"All the more reason they should know what they're getting into."

"You don't understand. On my planet, catfishing and scamming are perfectly respectable occupations. I almost took an internship in pyramid scheming, but it was too expensive, plus I had to recruit six other people. Besides, I like working with my hands. Pickpocketing, the occasional break-in."

"I admit, that sounds more interesting than my pre-GUPPEAS career." I'd worked in a canned-air factory, the only industry in my town. "But you're not getting out of this."

"I'll explain to Xerxzez that I need the money back."

"If they love you, they'll understand." As if I should be giving relationship advice. Speaking of which... "And you can't keep stealing that wedding ring. It belongs to Ambassador Dangere."

Frink gave me the ring. "You know I'm only doing this for you."

"What?"

"You don't want him to marry Richena Rossi."

I tried not to blush. "I've moved on from Beau. Isn't that what you all told me to do?"

"Sure, but you still care about him and you don't want him stuck with her. That would be horrible, for him and for you."

He had a point, but I didn't want to think about that. "First of all, a marriage isn't really about the ring."

Frink looked puzzled. "It is where I come from."

"I believe you. But it's not for you or me to decide what Beau does. You don't have to protect me."

"Of course I do. We're family on this ship."

"Wait, what?" Martian and I were family, but I'd never heard any of the crew talk like this.

"We're all family." Frink's voice had a sincerity I rarely heard. "Even Zeeko—he's like the weird cousin who shows up uninvited for a holiday meal and never leaves. And you're the super-young matriarch. I guess that makes Martian the uncle. We all take care of each other, because that's what families do." He left, taking my copy of *U, Robot* with him.

5

Assault With a Deadly Weapon Star

The hot fudge sundae in the chocolate shop was divine. I made a mental note to bring Randy here.

My companion was running late, so I pulled out my favorite book, *The Space-Faring Moron's Guide to Common Science Fiction Plot Devices*. It had a section on weapons, a subject I hadn't had to think about much before.

The typical science fiction universe has laser guns or blasters, as both handheld and ship-level weapons. Such weapons tend to result in total annihilation of the target, with no explanation of where all that matter went. Fortunately, villains are usually terrible shots who couldn't hit the ground if they tried. But don't wear a red shirt around them.

Occasionally a science fiction universe will have a Super-Weapon, capable of annihilating large population centers, planets, or the entire universe and any adjacent universes as well. Fortunately, such weapons always have a design flaw allowing one well-placed hero to destroy them with minimal weaponry of their own.

"Hello, Janet."

An Ursan man stood over me, his head covered in a mass of leafy green hair. He didn't look familiar, but he smiled and slid into the booth beside me. He caught the eye of one of the wait staff. "I'll have the chocolate lava cake, please."

"Hello, Nina," I said. I knew only one shape-shifter who could impersonate other species. Nina Mikeljohn was a forty-seventh-gender Jupiteran, the only kind that could change color and texture as well as shape. "Thought you were hanging around Pluto."

"The smuggling business is slow these days, since Pluto legalized chocolate." Nina grinned, aqua eyes glowing. "Nice to know you recognized me."

"I didn't at first. You were the human woman with the braids at the Counselor's banquet, right? And I was pretty sure the Jupiteran at the comedy club was you. You kept your eyes the same."

"I've tried different colors. But I've been told my eyes look...old." The server brought the cake to her. Him?

"This gets a little confusing with shape-shifters. If you're a Jupiteran woman disguised as an Ursan man, what's the right pronoun?"

"She."

"Always?"

"It's not about what I look like. It's about who I am."

That was refreshingly simple, considering Jupiterans changed their names every few decades out of boredom, and occasionally their species name as well. Nlubglub used to be named Gkuindpthweedl, but decided that was too unpronounceable for working with species who can't change the shape of their vocal cords at will.

"What brings you here?"

Nina gave me a cagey smile. "The lava cake. Have you tried it?" Jupiterans don't eat, normally. It took an amazingly skilled shape-shifter to give herself taste buds and a digestive system. From the look on her face, the chocolate was worth the trouble.

"I meant, here in the Pelican Nebula."

"Holofilms."

"Holofilms? Are you acting or directing?"

She laughed. "Neither. Jupiteran films are frowned upon here. Cygnoids claim their own are vastly superior. So Cygnoid cinema buffs buy Jupiteran holofilms from smugglers. The Counselor—did you know his real name is Grackle?—anyway, he's been trying to arrest me so he can give me a stern talking-to." She took another bite.

"I've been so bored lately; all the entertainment I get is dodging Cygnoid security and watching old Queelchu films. I'm tired of doing a solo operation. Have you given any more thought to working for me on the *Mariposa*? Offer's still open. Criminal record not a problem."

"Thanks, but I already have a job. And I'm not completely terrible at it now." After a moment, I added, "Most days."

"Good to know."

"We could use some help finding out more about this weapon the Cygnoids have. Like, what it does, how it's guarded."

"Sounds dangerous." Which, coming from her, wasn't necessarily a no. "You could wait for the Plutonians to do something stupid. Then you'll find out about the weapon when the Cygnoids use it on them."

"Nlubglub said the same thing. What is it with you Jupiterans and Plutonians? You've been getting into wars with each other since forever. Why?"

Her eyebrows came together as she pondered that, her leafy hair fluttering. "The first one was before my time. I've heard it was because they wanted to call us Jupiterists, and back then we called ourselves Jovians."

"A war over that? Ridiculous."

"Please." Her hedge-like eyebrows rose. "You Earthlings nearly melted your entire planet. You remake the same superhero movie every other year. You invented decaffeinated coffee. You don't get to talk about other species being ridiculous."

"We did fix the melting planet part. Mostly."

"Uh-huh." She scraped the last of the cake from her plate. "What's your plan for getting the Cygnoid weapon?"

The word *plan* might be overly generous. "You're a shape-shifter. You could disguise yourself as one of them."

"That would be quite an acting job. Like Queelchu in *The Neptune Adventure*." She giggled at the thought. "Do you know where this weapon is?"

"Uh...not yet."

"And once we find it, then what? Do I smuggle you in so you can use your magic anti-technology jinx on it?"

I pushed my empty bowl away, irritated. "Would everyone please stop saying that? I know technology sometimes gets weird around me, but—"

Outside the window, a floatcar flipped over and spilled four surprised Jupiterans onto the street.

"Oh, come on," I said. "I had nothing to do with that."

It took a moment to realize that Nina wasn't listening. Her attention was focused on two Cygnoid security officers walking into the shop. The Cygnoids sat down at the counter and ordered chocolate chip cookies.

"Gotta run," she said, and headed for the back door.

I watched her go, and then called Randy. "I've found this great chocolate shop. Want to join me tomorrow for a hot fudge sundae?"

He took a moment to respond. "I don't eat the same things Earthlings do. Could we do something else? There's a curling match tomorrow, GUPPEAS vs. the Cygnoid team. Want to check it out?"

"Sure." Something felt off, and I wasn't sure if it was because of Nina or Randy. "Sounds great."

The next day I met Randy at the curling rink. I was bundled up for the cold, but Randy met me in khakis and a short-sleeved shirt. Maybe his planet was prone to cold temperatures. I got a thermos of coffee from a vendor, and we settled in to watch the game.

Randy leaned forward, watching the players assemble on the ice. "How did you wind up a spaceship captain? That's quite an achievement at your age."

"There's a weird story behind it." There was a weird story behind most things in my life. This particular one started with me getting arrested, and I wasn't sure I wanted to go into that.

Wait. Why would I want to date someone if I had to hide things from him?

"The short version is, I caused a floatcar accident that destroyed City Hall, and they gave me the choice of joining GUPPEAS or going to jail. Pretty much everyone in GUPPEAS is there because of a minor crime. Hope you're not too shocked by my being a floatcar-accident felon."

Randy considered that. "As felons go, you don't seem very scary."

"I haven't been a captain for too long, but I'm really proud of the work we did on Pluto, getting them to reverse the ban on chocolate. And my crew and I opened negotiations with a newly discovered planet."

"Wow. My job in ship maintenance isn't nearly that exciting."

"There are times when I could use a little less excitement."

"Good thing we picked curling, then, and not Orion gladiator death-matches."

The first player slid a stone across the ice. Curling could be soothing to watch, seeing the teams strategize to land their stones on the target and knock their opponent's stones out of the way. I have no idea how anyone came up with using brooms to make a path for the stones, but it required both skill and artistry.

"Do they have curling on your planet?" I asked.

"Yes, it's very popular." Randy gestured toward the rink as the GUPPEAS team made a difficult shot. "That player's pretty good."

I nearly choked on my own heart. "He's the five-time GUPPEAS curling champion." Beau.

But I hadn't noticed him, while I was sitting here talking with Randy. That had to be a good sign, right? Beau was getting married, and I needed to get over him. And Randy hadn't done a single annoying thing so far.

Beau looked up. Did he just notice me in the stands?

A Cygnoid player took her shot and knocked Beau's stone out of the way. Beau said, "Nice shot," making the Cygnoid beam at him.

I still had to return the wedding ring. If it was still in my quarters and not on its way to Frink's long-distance love.

Beau's team lined up their next shot, and then the loudspeakers crackled. "Attention! This is Adequate Leader of Pluto. We have a ship overhead, armed with our latest weapon. And we're jealous that we didn't think of a cool name like Civilizer first, so ours is called the Big

Bleeper."

Another voice cut in. "Weren't we going to call it the Assault With a Deadly Weapon Star?"

"Come on," came a third voice. "Who names a deadly weapon Deadly Weapon? At least go with Maiming Star."

"Shut up, both of you." Adequate Leader's irritation was palpable. "The point is, we're going to destroy this so-called Civilizer. We're going to keep shooting until we find it, so you'll save a lot of trouble if you tell us where it is."

The spectators elbowed and shoved their way toward the exits. Wings whirred overhead as the Cygnoid team flew off. I caught a glimpse of Beau and his curling team reaching the door and escaping. Randy maneuvered through the crowd, pulling me along with him.

"Where are we going?" I shouted.

"Don't know. Your ship?"

"Okay." We weren't far from the dock, if we could get out of the stadium.

The Plutonian ship made a roaring noise, and a crystalline ray erupted. A moment later, everything and everyone was covered in a layer of ice. I had to smash the ice from my body and brush it off. On Randy, it melted away.

A voice from the ship said, "I don't think a curling rink was the best place to demonstrate an ice-based weapon."

"Shut up," said Adequate Leader's voice. "And we are not calling it the Maiming Star."

6

Angry. Not Just Disappointed.

Aboard the *Turkey*, I introduced Randy to the crew and we tried to figure out our next move.

"Do we need to do anything?" Lola asked. "This is on the Plutonians. Either the Cygnoids really have this super-weapon and they use it on the Plutonians, or they're bluffing. And we don't have any orders from GUPPEAS, beyond attending the conference."

Pilar fiddled with her glasses. "If we always waited for orders from GUPPEAS, I'd still be in that dungeon on Pluto." Pluto's previous ruler, known as Exalted Leader, hadn't taken kindly to her violating the ban on chocolate.

A suspicion nagged at me. "Nlubglub, you didn't put the Plutonians up to this, did you?"

"Of course not." They pointed eyestalks innocently up at the ceiling. "Why would Plutonians listen to a Jupiteran?"

Fair point. I said, "Shouldn't we protect the Plutonians? Seeing as we're a peace organization?"

"Protect them how?" Martian asked. "We don't know what the Civilizer does. And we don't have any weapons, because you won't let me invent any. Although I had a great idea for a cannon that shoots rotten zabbafruit." He pulled up a sketch to show me.

"Captain?" Frink looked up. "I've been monitoring communications, and the Cygnoids are broadcasting on every channel."

"Put it on the—"

Before I could finish the order, the Counselor's voice blared from the screen. "We warned you about this, Plutonians. We're not angry. We're just very disappointed."

"Why do people say that?" Zeeko shook his head. "It's never true."

"Quiet," Lola hissed.

"Plutonians, you shall now suffer the full fury of the Civilizer. As this is your first offense, we shall set it at the lowest setting, Level 3."

Martian asked, "Why would the lowest setting be 3 instead of—"

He was interrupted by a confusion of cries and wails from the Plutonians. "Make it stop!" "Get away!" One was sobbing, another moaning. The loudest voice might have been Adequate Leader, but it was hard to tell. "It's not our fault! That purple Jupiteran talked us into attacking you."

I shot a suspicious look at Nlubglub, whose face flattened into a poor imitation of innocence.

"I didn't tell them to do anything, Captain. When I ran into them at the billiard parlor, I may have casually suggested that if Plutonians are really as tough as they claim to be, they shouldn't have any problem standing up to a species claiming to be peacemakers. But anything they did was strictly their own choice."

"Anyway," Lola cut in, "this gives us information about the Civilizer. The Plutonians are still alive. The weapon's capable of reaching through the shields on a ship. And either it's got an amazing range, or it's nearby."

"We don't know how it affects non-Plutonians," Martian said. "It would help if we had more information about exactly what the weapon did."

"The Plutonians may not care to talk to us." I was still glaring at Nlubglub.

"I could offer them my services," Pilar suggested. "They might be glad to see a doctor right now."

Frink added, "We could spy on one of the Cygnoids, like the Counselor's assistant."

"We need a tracking device." Lola smacked Martian's arm.

"Invent one."

Martian rubbed his arm. "Those have already been invented. But they're illegal."

All eyes turned to Frink.

"I might have a couple stashed away."

Zeeko said, "Why don't we ask the Cygnoids about the weapon?"

I glanced over at Randy. I was a bit embarrassed to have him here, watching my crew bicker, and Zeeko sounding ridiculous as usual.

Randy said, "Has anyone tried? Some species will give you a straight answer."

I tried to organize my thoughts. "Let's use multiple approaches. Pilar, you talk to the Plutonians. That won't be too traumatic for you after your last encounter with that species?"

Pilar wiped her glasses and put them back on. "I'll manage."

"Martian, get any data you can find about that encounter with the weapon."

Martian was already checking his instruments. "Radiation levels, energy type, sound wave patterns, I'm on it."

"And someone needs to talk to the Cygnoids." No one volunteered. "I'll text Ambassador Dangere."

I looked for a way to salvage a date that was on my top ten list for disasters, none of which was Randy's fault. Or mine either, come to think of it.

"Would you like to see the ship?"

His face lit up. "Sure."

I reached for the door. The handle broke off in my hand.

"The committee couldn't agree on a name for the ship, so they compromised on *Cosmic Old York Nerthus Turkey*." I was already questioning whether giving Randy this tour was going to scare him off. My ship wasn't a shiny new model like Richena's dragon-shaped space yacht. The *Turkey* was cramped, ugly, and constantly in need of repairs.

"What's a Nerthus?" We rounded a corner so tight that we had to go single file.

"A legendary goddess from Scandinavia, which is a part of Earth that's almost as cold as Pluto." I'd shown him the bridge, engineering, mess hall, and view room. The latter was less impressive when we weren't looking down on a planet. "And a turkey is a bird. The ship sort of looks like one."

"Birds get this big on your planet?"

"What? No. Just the shape." We passed a section of crew quarters, and Frink emerged from his room. Through the open door, I spotted a long-handled battle-axe next to an expensively framed Ursan painting.

"Uh…hello, Captain. I can explain."

I put on my most authoritative tone. "Frink, put the axe back in Lola's quarters. You didn't take her meditation crystal, did you?"

"I wouldn't touch her meditation crystal. She's scary when she doesn't have it."

"Yeah, put back whatever else you took before the non-scary Lola uses that axe on you."

We waited until Frink emerged from Lola's room empty-handed. Randy asked, "I thought GUPPEAS didn't allow weapons?"

"It's decorative." At least, that was what she'd told us.

My beepity-beeper signaled an incoming call. Beau. I picked up.

"Hello, Janet. I mean, Captain. I've set up a meeting with the Counselor tomorrow, to try to talk the Cygnoids out of their plans. Can you accompany me?"

My heart sped up. I tried to make it behave. "What about Richena?"

"She…isn't available."

I spent a very mean moment fantasizing that Richena had fallen out of one of those giant trees. "Sure, I'll be there. Oh, and I do have your ring. I'll return it to you then."

As I disconnected the call, Frink said, "Uh, actually…"

I gave him an incredulous look. Frink went back into his quarters, retrieved the ring, and handed it to me. He also returned a wallet to a surprised-looking Randy. "Sorry. Habit."

"Make sure everything's still in it." I led Randy down the hall. "There's not much more to see, except the shuttle bay."

I opened the door to the shuttle bay. Despite having been iced over by Plutonians and robbed by my pilot, Randy still seemed in a pleasant mood. He asked, "Where's the shuttle?"

"On Earth, getting repaired. So the shuttle bay doesn't get used much." I pointed to a tarp-covered blob in the back. "There's a float-car in case we need to get around on the planet."

"What's this?" Randy indicated a small oblong device with a blinking orange light on top.

What was it? I had no idea. There was a tablet-sized screen next to it with mathematical codes scrolling past. I walked over to look at it. "Martian uses this area to test new inventions. Maybe he—"

The machine surged. My feet went in different directions, and I landed hard on a sheet of ice that hadn't been there a moment earlier.

Martian ran in behind us, staying upright as he slid over to his machine. "What did you do to it?"

"Nothing. Why are we on ice? Did the Plutonians attack again?"

Randy walked over to help me up. The ice melted underneath me, soaking my uniform as I scrambled to my feet.

Martian fiddled with the controls. "No. I had the same basic idea as them, but mine's a more useful invention. It creates a sheet of ice from moisture in the air. I figured we could use the shuttle bay for curling practice." He looked up. "That's weird. How come it's melted around you two, and nowhere else?"

My socks were sopping wet. I hated wet socks. "How should I know?"

"Right." Martian frowned at the tablet, scrolling through equations. "By the way, did you get that message from Mom and Dad?"

"Haven't checked messages." A chill ran through me that had nothing to do with the ice. "Is everything okay?"

"They're being deployed away from Lyra, but they haven't gotten their orders yet."

Randy walked past me to scrutinize Martian's tablet. "I think I saw your mistake. Scroll back. There." He pointed to a column of figures. "You forgot to carry the two."

Martian whistled softly. "Good catch. Thanks."

I told Randy, "We should probably call it a day. I have a big meeting with the Counselor tomorrow."

"Okay." He took my hand and we walked toward the exit. "See you again soon?"

All the disasters today, and he was still interested? Maybe I was doing something right after all. "Absolutely."

We reached the entrance. Maybe we'd get to kiss this time?

My beepity-beeper announced an urgent message from Pilar, and the letters appeared between my face and Randy's. *You need to talk to these Plutonians. Come here ASAP.*

I gave Randy an apologetic smile.

I tried to call back, but Pilar wasn't responding, so I left a message and hurried to where the Plutonian ship was docked. It didn't appear damaged, as far as I could tell.

The Plutonian who let me aboard was unusually pale green, and her antennae kept rattling against each other. I was ushered to Sick Bay, where I found Pilar with Adequate Leader and several other Plutonians.

Pilar was leading them in a guided meditation. "Picture someplace pleasant, like a really cold, barren spot on Pluto, with nothing growing but mold... Breathe out the stress, breathe in peace... Feel that soothing, bracing cold... Breathe..."

Adequate Leader interrupted, "How about we picture a dark nasty dungeon, filled with Cygnoids that we can smack until their feathers fall off?"

I cleared my throat. "Hello, Your Adequacy." His real name, I remembered with an effort, was Byufulus Fedderbang. "I hope no one's seriously injured."

He looked up from his chair, antennae quivering. "You have no idea what we've been through."

"And it was all that purple Jupiteran's fault," one of the others added.

I was tempted to defend my crew member, but this didn't seem like a good moment to admit to knowing Nlubglub. "What can you tell us about the weapon?"

When none of the Plutonians responded, Pilar began. "It's psychological torture, Captain. Brutal in its efficiency."

Adequate Leader shuddered. "It forces you to relive one of the most mortifying, most humiliating moments of your life."

"It embarrasses you?" This took me a second. "That's it?"

"That's it?" Adequate Leader leapt to his feet, antennae straight up. "Why don't you tell us all about the most humiliating thing that ever happened to you?"

"Don't leave out any details," added another Plutonian.

The most humiliating moment of my life? Would that be the prom with Pietro, when I wore a dress with a computer chip programmed for the latest dances, and it gave a new meaning to "wardrobe malfunction"? Or the time that...

Oh.

That.

"I see your point," I said. "This isn't what I expected when they told us about the weapon."

"Shame is a powerful emotion," Pilar said. "Most species will go to great lengths to avoid feeling it."

"They told us they were starting with Level 3," another Plutonian added. "Our third most embarrassing experience. I don't want to think about what Level 2 and Level 1 would be like." He shuddered, and Pilar gave him a tranquilizer.

"There was something else," another one added. "They said they were working on a Level Zero. But what could be worse than your worst memory?"

"We have to get rid of this so-called Civilizer," I said.

"Oh no." Adequate Leader sat back down. "No way are we risking going through that again. We're going to destroy the Big Bleeper and the rest of our weapons."

"We'll have to make all those changes the Cygnoids demanded," said the Plutonian who'd escorted me in. "Stop banning mystery novels. Stop using the slogan *Realest of the real planets*. Raise the planetary temperature. You Earthlings know how to do that, right?"

"That's a terrible idea." I looked to Adequate Leader. "We have to stop the Cygnoids. We can work together."

"Thanks for loaning us your doctor. But you're on your own. It was bad enough having to relive the time that I spoiled a romantic moment by calling my wife Queelchu." Realization crept across Adequate Leader's face like a Saturnian micro-rodent across a cheese wheel. "Wait, did I actually tell you that?" He smacked himself on the antenna. "That's gotta be my fourth most embarrassing experience."

"It's all right." Pilar had a wonderfully soothing voice, accustomed to calming distraught patients. "You were so traumatized, you had no idea what you were saying. Captain, we'd better go."

As soon as we were outside the Plutonian ship, Nlubglub called me on the beepity-beeper. "How badly were the Plutonians injured? Are they dead?"

"We'll discuss that when I get back to the ship." I was angry. Not just disappointed. "Nlubglub, if I catch you messing with Plutonians like that again, I'm going to tell the Vegans you invited them over for breakfast."

7

If You Were a Spaceship

Beau and I rode the elevator up to the Counselor's office, located at the top of the giant tree that housed the Great Hall. "Almost forgot." I handed over the ring. "Sorry about Frink. He can't help himself."

"Thanks." Our fingers brushed as he took the ring from me. "I'll try to guard it better."

We stepped off the elevator, to a polished wood floor and ivy-covered walls. Grebe greeted us with enthusiasm. "Captain, that selfie of us together got so many likes. My friends keep asking if you made the camera explode, ha ha." After a moment, he added, "I mean from your technology-slayer thing, not because you look bad."

"I know. It's fine." I tried to walk past.

Grebe didn't move. "There was this funny bit in Pietro's column about you; did you see it?"

I waited a moment, then took a tone that I hoped would end the topic. "No."

"Oh, you have to see it. Wait, I'll find it." He scrolled through a sparkly phone.

The Counselor appeared in the doorway. "Grebe, leave the captain alone. I'm sure she has more pressing concerns right now."

"Right. Of course." Grebe escorted us into the Counselor's chamber.

I nearly fell through the floor.

"Floor" wasn't the right word, in a building constructed around a tree. While the area outside the Counselor's chamber had a real floor, the inside had an interlocking set of branches, with nothing covering the gaps in between. Looking down, I could see other layers of branches, down to a barely visible ground level far below.

Beau grabbed my arm to steady me, and for one terrifying moment I thought we were both going to crash through. Then I found my footing. "Thanks."

Was it my imagination, or did Beau hesitate before letting go of my arm? He must have been making sure I was safe.

The Counselor fluttered to a nest of twigs at the center of the room, sat down, and smoothed his silver feathers. His cape continued to flap on its own. "What was it you wanted to discuss?"

I wanted to say *What else could we possibly want to discuss besides your insane plan to control the galaxy?*

Fortunately, Beau spoke before I did. "We're concerned about your peace plan. A lot of species are interpreting it more as a conquest plan, and they're not taking it very well."

The Counselor gave a dismissive wing-wave. "Nonsense. Species have been shooting at each other for millennia, and all it's ever brought them is death and destruction."

"I noticed you included several species in this conference who are entirely peaceful." How did Beau learn to keep his voice so calm? I'd have to ask him to teach me that. "The Saturnians, for instance, have lived without violence for centuries."

"Mostly because their transportation system is so inefficient that their armies gave up before they ever reached each other. And have you seen their architecture? So dreary. And they have far too many telemarketers."

"I don't disagree about the telemarketers, but what if that's the way the Saturnians like it? What if they find their architecture homey and unobtrusive?"

"And they invented lawyers for the sole purpose of banning them. More primitive cultures always resist change, but they'll see that it's for their own good. Take your captain here, for instance. While I'm sure she may like that garish uniform, once we replace it with a more elegant design, you will see that it's really for the best. And that whole business of Earthlings choosing their own mates—how well has that worked out for you?"

Considering how that had worked out for me, I didn't have an answer.

"Respectfully, I believe you're missing the point." Beau's self-control never wavered, but I could hear the tightness in his throat. "If we make mistakes, they're still our own mistakes. We're able to learn from them because we're free to make better choices for ourselves. Look at what's happening on Cassiopeia VII right now. They're having a robot uprising, because the Cassiopeians wouldn't grant the robots the freedoms they wanted. Do you want to spend all your time putting down rebellions because you want to tell another species how to dress or what music they can listen to?" Beau pulled up some shaky footage on his beepity-beeper, a crowded street full of figures shooting lasers at each other.

I watched, open-mouthed. "That's Cassiopeia VII?" Randy's planet.

"Yes." Beau switched it off. "This footage was smuggled out anonymously and released this morning."

Another wing-wave from the Counselor. "They don't know what's good for them."

"And you do? Really?" I hadn't meant to say it, but the words burst forth like an antimatter leak. "Ambassador Dangere and I can't fly, but it didn't cross your mind to have this meeting someplace where we'd be comfortable. We're standing here wobbling back and forth, trying not to fall off the branch. You can't be bothered to consider anyone's point of view other than your own." A handful of leaves fluttered loose from the ceiling and landed on my head.

Despite that, Beau looked impressed. "Janet, the Counselor's wasting our time." He took my arm and helped me climb along the branch, back out the door.

At the entrance, Grebe looked up from his phone. "There you are. Hope the meeting went well?" Before I could answer, Grebe shoved the phone in my face. "Here's that column of Pietro's that I told you about."

I spotted my name and the words *dating profile* before wincing and gently pushing the phone out of my way. "Grebe, I can't help wondering. Is there anyone you want a selfie with, that you haven't been able to get?"

Grebe's dark eyes shone with excitement. "Well, the Plutonian curling team, of course. But my absolute dream? Queelchu."

"The Jupiteran actress? That's funny—I've heard she's here on Cygnus IV right now."

"Really?" Cygnoids didn't have auras like Venusians, but Grebe's face could have lit up a city block.

"Might be a rumor," I added quickly. "I'll try to find out."

Beau and I walked out together. He kept his voice low. "Thanks for saying that to the Counselor. I was about to explode."

"You? That's hard to believe."

I sent a text to Nina, asking if she'd given any more thought to being the next Queelchu. It was only later that I noticed: the Counselor had asked how it worked out when Earthlings chose our mates. And Beau hadn't mentioned his impending marriage.

I texted Randy that evening, with no response. In the morning I had two more scam calls, and a message from Martian. *Repairs are taking longer than I thought. Don't worry, I'm on it. And don't read Pietro's column. Seriously, don't.*

I held out for seventeen minutes, and then I read Pietro's column.

Looking to have your car, your computer, and all the other tech in your life spontaneously disassemble itself? Good news: Jam-it Delane has a dating profile up on LuckyStar. It says she likes long walks on the beach (as far from civilization as possible), chocolate (might want to go easy on that, just saying), and curling. (Remember that time she used a mechanical broom? Here's a picture of what was left of the rink, if you missed it.)

"My team won that match!" I shouted at no one.

The computer giggled.

"Computer, did you have something you wanted to say to me?"

The computer adopted a blandly polite tone that still managed to sound smug. "Incoming message from your mother."

I played the message. *Hi, Janet and Martian. Wanted to let you know that we're being deployed to Cassiopeia VII to deal with a robot uprising. I'm sure it'll be fine—we've worked with robots before. We used to have one for a commanding officer. Dad says hello. Will be in touch soon.*

I set down the beepity-beeper and paced the length of my tiny quarters. This wasn't the first time my parents had gone into a dangerous situation. But that footage from Cassiopeia VII had left me shaken.

The computer changed the motivational poster on the view-screen. Now it said, *The Saturnian symbol for crisis means "danger-ous opportunity." In Venusean, it means "discounted glittery hand-bags." In Vegan, it means "food," but so does most of their vocabulary.*

Not helping. I reached for my copy of *The Space-Faring Moron's Guide to Common Science Fiction Plot Devices.* There was a section on robots.

There are two kinds of robots: good ones who want to be people, and bad ones who want to kill people. How can a robot be bad? Duh, they're programmed by people, and there's no shortage of bad ones. No one ever writes about well-adjusted robots who like long walks on the beach.

I flipped a few more pages, and discovered a section on parents.

If you are in a young adult story, get the parents as far away as possible, as quickly as possible. Otherwise they're likely to die. Parents in YA stories have disturbingly short life expectancies, and usually cannot obtain insurance.

My stomach tightened. I wanted to send a message back to my parents, but couldn't think what to say except *Be careful.*

And because I'd take any distraction from thinking about that, I read the rest of Pietro's column. The last paragraph was a bit of self-promotion.

I've been hired on as a creative consultant for a reality TV pilot here on Cygnus IV. The details are very hush-hush, but the producer is a certain selfie-loving assistant to the Counselor, and the first episode will focus on humans. Couples are encouraged to apply—stay tuned.

Grebe was making a television show? And what did Pietro mean by consulting?

Wheels turned in my head. Grebe was probably the best source of information besides the Counselor. Reality TV sounded like the perfect forum to get people talking with their guard down.

An incoming call buzzed. I almost ignored it, then saw Randy's face on the screen. His voice sounded uncharacteristically tentative. "Hi, thanks for your message last night. I saw the footage from Cassiopeia."

"It's a robot uprising?"

"Yes. They wanted back wages and weekends off. They were negotiating with Leader Dessimal, but then all the printers on the planet jammed at once, and she accused the robots of sabotaging them. She threatened to cut off their power supply, and now everyone's shooting at each other. I was lucky to get out."

I started to tell him my parents were headed there, then changed my mind. I didn't know Randy that well, and it felt wrong to dump my problems on him. "Maybe GUPPEAS could help. Send in someone skilled with both diplomacy and technology."

"That rules you out," said a snarky voice.

Randy blinked. "Who was that?"

"My computer," I told him. "Never mind it. How are you doing? It must be hard, being so far away from home."

"Yes. I came to the peace conference hoping the Cygnoids would help, but their so-called peace plan would enslave all our planets."

Inspiration struck. "This may be the weirdest idea ever for a third date, but would you like to do some undercover work?" I explained my plan.

"Love to," Randy said. "And it can't turn out any crazier than having Plutonians using their ice weapon at the curling match, right?"

The computer giggled again. "Sure it could."

I glared it into silence.

By the next afternoon, we were in the TV building, constructed around a tree with pine-like needles. At least we were on the ground floor and not up in the branches. Grebe apparently spent a lot of time here, as the front desk in the lobby was decorated with selfies of him and various interplanetary celebrities. We were escorted to a sound stage, where a harried-looking Grebe was flapping around, checking in with stagehands and film crew, and moving chairs from one spot to another.

I'd already pestered Randy with every question I could think of about Cassiopeia VII: what the robots were like (pretty much like the people who'd programmed them), how bad the violence had gotten (only isolated areas when he'd left, but spreading), and how much danger any military arrivals might be in (no way to know). There was nothing I could do from here, except try to weasel information out of Grebe about the Civilizer.

"This is great," Grebe said, pausing to sink into a chair next to Randy and me. "I was trying to figure out how to get enough volunteers, and now I have four already. Pietro was right about putting it in his column." Grebe pulled out a pocket mirror and fluffed his eyebrows. "Does my beak look too shiny? Are my feathers curled right?"

"You look great. Did you say four volunteers?" I looked around.

"Are they not here yet? Oh no, this is going to be a disaster."

"Grebe?"

I froze at the sound of Beau's voice.

Beau shut the door behind him. "This must be the right place."

Grebe jumped up. "Oh good, you're here. Where's Captain Rossi?"

"She couldn't make it." There was an unfamiliar edge to Beau's voice. "Sorry." Had he and Richena had a lovers' quarrel? I reminded myself that it was none of my business. I was here with Randy.

"Only three humans? Oh no. I'll have to talk to the writers about tweaking the concept." Grebe flew from the room.

I introduced Randy to Beau. "I saw you at the curling match," Randy said. "Janet mentioned you were the GUPPEAS champion."

"How did you wind up here?" I added.

Beau smiled. "I saw the teaser about this show in Pietro's column, and I thought it would be a way to get close to Grebe and see if he lets any information slip about the weapon."

"Wow." Randy looked from Beau to me. "You two think alike."

Grebe fluttered back in. "The writers are reworking the script."

I blinked. "I thought reality shows were supposed to be unscript-ed."

Grebe gave me an annoyed look. "The working title is 'Lovebirds,' and it's all about matching contestants with the perfect mate."

Randy said, "I'm Cassiopeian—"

"It's a dating show?" Beau took a step back, looking embarrassed. "I didn't realize that. I'm engaged, so obviously I wouldn't—"

"This is just a demo, to give the Counselor a feel for what the show will be like." Grebe's voice rose to a whine. "Please, you have to help me. The Counselor thinks we should do a dance-off instead. But a dating show with humans would be great. You're so funny."

My mouth gave a skeptical twist. "I don't know what Cygnoids consider funny."

"You're funniest when you don't know you're being funny." Grebe checked with the camera people, fussing over angles. "Janet, you take the center seat, and Beau and Randy take the side seats." We took the chairs as indicated. "The idea is, Janet, you have to choose between the two of them for a date."

My mouth went dry.

Grebe went blithely on. "In the first part, I'm going to ask you questions. Don't think about it; say the first thing that comes to mind. Ready?"

"No," I said.

Grebe was thrown off stride. "What?"

"You said to answer the question without thinking about it."

"Not that one." Grebe pulled out the mirror again, and plucked a stray feather above one ear. "First question is for Beau. What would you say is Janet's most attractive quality?"

My face flushed as I tried to keep from looking at him.

"I don't know Janet that well." Beau sounded like he was stalling for time. Maybe he couldn't think of anything attractive about me? "But I'm impressed with how much she cares about her crew, and it's obvious they feel the same way about her. And I like the way she takes charge, even when you drop her into an insane situation."

Take charge? Me? I barely thought of myself as a real captain. Should I be taking charge right now? "Grebe, it seems like we ought to be able to ask you questions too. So that we can get to know our host better and make it a better TV show."

Beau followed my lead. "For instance, where would you say you spend most of your time?"

Grebe brushed off the question. "The host part is later. Right now, it's Randy's turn to answer."

"Janet's most attractive quality?"

"No, having the same question would be too easy. Your question is: What's Janet's least attractive quality?"

"That's not fair," Randy said. "How do I have a chance if he gets to say good things about her and I don't?"

"Don't worry, he'll get some terrible questions. We don't want to be too predictable."

Randy thought for a moment. "Janet seems to have kind of a hostile relationship with her ship's computer. I can't figure out what that's about."

"You'd have to ask the computer," I said.

"You're all wrong," came a smug voice. Pietro strolled onto the stage.

"This is the kind of twist that will have the audience on the edge of their branches." Grebe hopped up and down with excitement. "You think you know what's happening, and then the ex walks in."

"No," I said. "I never thought I knew what was happening."

Grebe wasn't listening. "Pietro, tell them why they're wrong."

"Janet's least attractive quality is when she tries to dance." He wasn't going to show that video clip, was he? It wasn't the top of my most embarrassing moments, but it was on the list. "And her best quality is recognizing true talent when she sees it. Janet was always my biggest fan when we were together."

"That's not quite the way I remember it." Because Pietro's biggest fan, no contest, was Pietro.

"Next question." Grebe either didn't notice my annoyance, or decided it would bring in ratings. "Randy, where would you take Janet to dinner on your ideal date?"

Randy shifted uncomfortably. "We don't eat the same foods. I'd take Janet to that chocolate shop that she likes, and try to make good conversation while she enjoys her dessert."

Beau gave him a nod. "Solid answer."

Grebe went on. "Beau, what's the one terrible secret you wouldn't want Janet to know about you?"

Beau looked flummoxed for a moment. "I…I'm not really a terrible-secret kind of guy… Wait, here's one. I've lost my fiancée's wedding ring three times already."

Pietro smirked. "The fact that you have a fiancée would be the first problem."

"If this was a real dating show, yes." Beau turned his attention back to Grebe. "You have to know something about dating to run a show like this. Grebe, are you in a relationship right now?" Clever: if Grebe had a partner, they would be another possible source of information.

Grebe squawked, "No time. Too busy taking care of the Counselor's appointments and getting this show together. I need to find more contestants who are looking for a date."

I started to ask what kind of appointments for the Counselor, but Pietro interrupted. "You could try that LuckyStar website. They get the most ridiculous profiles." He held up his phone. "Here's one from an Ursan guy, promising to marry whoever sends him the perfect diamond ring."

I tried not to groan. Time to have another talk with Frink about his romance scams. I looked at Pietro's screen and noticed another picture. "Pietro, you have a profile on LuckyStar?"

Pietro snatched his phone away. "That's for research. Who had the next question? Must be Randy."

Grebe shuffled through a handful of index cards. "Randy, what's the one terrible secret you wouldn't want Janet to know about you?"

Randy's eyes widened. It was nothing obvious, but I got the feeling he was about to panic. Didn't he know nobody had to tell the truth on a reality show?

Pietro missed all that, and asked Grebe, "I thought you were giving them different questions?"

"Oh. Right." Grebe went on to the next card. "What would you say is the key to a good relationship?"

"Radical honesty," Randy said.

"Now the competitors get to ask Janet questions," Grebe chirped. "Beau, you first."

Beau looked surprised at the shift in the rules, but after a few moments to think, he came up with, "Describe your ideal date."

"Come on," Grebe said, "can't you come up with something more unusual? Like, if you were a spaceship, what kind of spaceship would you be?"

"I like Beau's question," I said. "The best date I ever had was very spur-of-the-moment. We practiced curling under a bright green moon, and talked about our families, and had coffee."

Everyone looked at me expectantly.

"That was it. He was great company, and we had a meaningful conversation."

Grebe looked annoyed. Should I have made up something weirder, or sexier? That evening with Beau was priceless to me, even if it didn't happen in his timeline. Pietro also looked annoyed, probably because my answer wasn't about him.

Grebe looked at Randy. "Your turn. Ask Janet a question."

"Um..." Randy's forehead wrinkled. "If you were a spaceship, what kind of spaceship would you be?"

"I've heard that on Cassiopeia VII they have ships made of living matter. That's the kind I'd be." I hoped that wouldn't sound too much like I was trying to ingratiate myself, but it was the first thing I remembered about Randy's planet. And a spaceship that replaced technology with biology sounded perfect for me.

Pietro said, "I should get to ask a question too."

Grebe looked a little miffed to be thrown off script, but gestured for Pietro to continue.

Pietro's aura wavered a little, unexpectedly. "Do you regret any of your past breakups?"

Did I? I regretted not being with Beau, but technically in this timeline it hadn't happened, so we never got a breakup. As for breaking up with Pietro...

"No." I held his gaze steadily. "I don't regret any relationship I've had, and there are always good memories. But some people are wrong for each other. Star-crossed. Personality-crossed. Whatever. If nothing else, any past mistakes might keep me from making the same mistakes in the future."

Pietro looked away, and for a moment I felt bad for him. Then I remembered that he'd been the one who broke up with me, and he'd mocked me mercilessly in his blog afterward.

Grebe said, "We're done with the question portion. Next is the combat portion."

Beau, Randy, and I spoke at once. "What?"

"The combat portion, to impress your possible mate. Your choice of weapons includes a curling broom, an eggbeater, a pile of jelly beans, or a stun gun."

"Don't pick the stun gun." Pietro smirked. "You know how Janet is with technology."

"What?" Randy looked at him blankly.

Beau said, "I'm from a peace organization. And so is Janet."

"This is all ridiculous," I said. And it wasn't getting us any closer to the Civilizer. "I think we're done here."

Grebe nearly screeched in alarm. "But we haven't gotten to the kissing contest yet!"

That gave me pause. An excuse to kiss both Randy and Beau? But then I saw Beau's face, and he looked mortified. This wasn't what he'd agreed to, and he shouldn't have to get stuck with explaining it to Richena afterward.

Randy didn't look particularly horrified at the prospect of kissing me. Good to know.

"Grebe," I said, "I realize you don't know a lot about kissing, what with the beaks and all. Kissing is something people do when they really want to. Otherwise it doesn't feel good."

"I watched a lot of human television to prepare for this show, and it's, like, nonstop kissing. Even if it looks like cannibalism."

"Television isn't real life. Especially not reality television."

Beau added, "How are you going to have kissing on the show when that's one of the things the Counselor was going to ban on Earth?"

"Was that on the list of rules for Earth? I thought it was for Kappa Leporis." Grebe was distracted by a message pinging on his communicator. "Oh no! Everyone, wait here. I'll be right back."

I casually moved in front of the door. "Is everything okay? Did the Plutonians attack again?"

"Worse. My stylist sprained a wing. Who's going to fluff my feathers? I need to make some calls." Grebe pushed past me and flew off.

I looked over at Pietro. "How did you get mixed up in this?"

"The Counselor loves reality TV. They're thinking about using my idea for a show about writers."

Randy looked surprised. "People watch shows about writers?"

"Not yet, they don't." Pietro pulled out his phone and scrolled. "Still need a topic for this week's column."

I said casually, "I heard that Queelchu was here on Cygnus IV. Something about a surprise guest appearance at that big curling match this week."

Beau gave me a curious look. Maybe he remembered Grebe gushing about wanting a selfie with Queelchu. "You know, for all their complaining about Jupiteran cinema, there seem to be a lot of Queelchu fans here on Cygnus."

Pietro's face lit up. "I could put an item in my column about that. Maybe I can score an interview with her."

Grebe reappeared. "We're done for today. I'll escort you all out."

"I got a tidbit for my column," Pietro said. "Be sure to read it this week."

As we walked, Randy whispered, "Pietro really thinks that Queelchu story was his idea?"

"That was pretty much our whole relationship," I whispered back.

8

Last Year's Water Dancing Shoes

I arrived early at the curling rink and tried a few practice shots. There was no one to sweep the ice, so I concentrated on sliding the stones one by one, arranging them into a pattern around the target. The object was to get one stone closest to the center, with extra points for each additional stone closer than the opponents' stones. But the way to succeed wasn't always to aim for the center. Set up the stones, anticipate the opponent's moves, knock theirs out of the way, and then take that final shot.

Sort of like making a plan to get at the Civilizer.

A stone whirled by and crashed into mine. A team of Vegans was setting up next to me. I retreated into the stands, trying to look unappetizing.

I checked my beepity-beeper for messages. Nothing from my parents. They probably hadn't gotten to Cassiopeia yet. There were a few messages from various LuckyStar patrons, asking about my income, my fertility, and my reason for not responding within five minutes of the first message. Delete, delete, delete. It was a wonder anyone managed to connect at all. I looked again at the picture of the LuckyStar founders, Fibby (a Plutonian politician) and Queelchu (a has-been Jupiteran actress), and wondered if anyone would ever smile at me with the adoration they obviously felt for each other.

"What's that you're looking at?"

Queelchu was standing over me, identical in every way to the dark green face on my screen.

"Hi, Nina." I moved over to make room for the shape-shifter. "It's a dating site. Ever used one?"

"No. I only date other Jupiterans. Other species are too short-lived."

I hadn't considered that point. "But what if you pick the wrong one, and you're stuck together for centuries?"

"Jupiteran divorce lawyers make a very good living. I've already dated most of them, at one time or another."

An ear-shattering screech pierced the air. For a moment I thought the Plutonians were back, with some sort of auditory weapon. Then I looked up.

Grebe landed in front of us, screaming with joy at the sight of Queelchu. Planting the item in Pietro's column had brought the desired effect. "I can't believe it's really you. Can I get a selfie with you?"

"Of course." Nina struck a pose, wielding a broom like the trophy in Queelchu's movie *To All the Curls I've Loved Before.*

Grebe snapped excitedly. "Wait, my beak looks weird in that one. No, wait, my feathers are ruffled. There, perfect."

"I think I've seen you before," Nina said. "When the Counselor made the big announcement."

"Yes, I'm the Counselor's assistant."

"That must be pretty overwhelming, such important work. Most people couldn't handle a job like that."

"It's a big responsibility," Grebe agreed. "Taking care of his appointments, making sure the tiny fan under his cape makes it flutter dramatically, and keeping the Counselor away from all the people who are upset about the peace plan."

"Especially with that new weapon." Nina kept her tone casual. "It's all anybody's talking about."

"I know people are upset." Grebe spoke quickly, as if expecting an argument. "Everyone will understand, once they see it's for the best."

"People don't always know what's good for them. They don't

understand the big picture."

"Exactly!" Grebe's relief at hearing agreement was as palpable as the ice underneath us. "It's very cygnane."

It took me a minute to figure out that was the Cygnoid equivalent of "humane." Meanwhile, another Vegan walked in front of me, and I missed the next few exchanges between Nina and Grebe. When they came back into view, they were still talking about the Civilizer.

"Do you have any selfies with it?"

"Oh, no." Grebe's voice dripped with disappointment. "I couldn't do that. Security reasons."

"Are you sure? Because I would love to take a picture with it. That would be my most prized possession."

"The Counselor would never allow it."

Nina leaned in close. "The Counselor doesn't have to know."

Temptation and duty fought a perilous battle on Grebe's face. "No. It wouldn't be right." Grebe stood up and flexed his wings. "I need to go."

"Okay." Nina's smile didn't change. "The offer to join me at curling practice is still open."

"Thanks." Grebe flapped away.

Nina climbed up the bleachers and slid into the seat beside me. "That went well."

"It did?"

"Yeah. Grebe never noticed when I slipped the tracking device into his feathers." Nina sent the codes to my beepity-beeper. "Good luck."

Back at the ship, the crew and I monitored Grebe's movements for a few days. Some of his haunts were expected: the Great Hall, the Counselor's residence, the TV studio, the curling rink (repeatedly asking for Queelchu, without success). Others were quick, occasional stops: coffee shops and a gallery that displayed millions of selfies.

There was one unlabeled building where Grebe spent a lot of

time.

We waited for a day when Grebe went there after dark. The crew and I landed on the roof in a floatcar, and we crept over to a skylight. The tinted glass was too dark to see inside.

"There's a door here," Lola said. "It's a little tight, but the captain and Nlubglub should be able to fit through."

Usually I don't think of my small size as an asset, but today it worked out. "Frink, can you get the lock?"

Frink snorted. "Does a Plutonian cheat at curling?" He had it open in a moment. Nlubglub stepped through the shadowy doorway.

And immediately plunged ten meters to the floor below, with me right behind. If I hadn't landed on top of Nlubglub's rubbery body, I'd have broken my neck. Fortunately, Jupiterans are almost indestructible. I looked up to see that the door led to nothing but a perch, which was all an avian species like the Cygnoids would need.

Mirrored walls on every side showed an endless number of Grebes, each looking up in surprise from a raised chair where another Cygnoid was rearranging his feathers. "You use this salon too?" I was saved from answering by a coughing fit, as the chemical smell assailed my senses.

The stylist looked at me skeptically. "I've never tried to do those kinds of feathers. What do you call them? Hairs?" Her feathers were pale orange, sculpted into points and tipped with golden glitter.

"Yes," I choked out, getting up and trying to act nonchalant. "I already have a stylist." Doing hair was one of the few things Zeeko never screwed up. "We, ah, seem to be at the wrong address. I didn't see a sign outside."

The stylist looked affronted. "This is an exclusive salon! Customers by referral only! We have no need to advertise."

"We were looking for the billiard parlor." Nlubglub wobbled to their feet, moving unusually slowly. "I was going to teach the captain some of my winning technique."

"Three doors down." Grebe pointed. "And, ah, could you not mention this to anyone? They all think my feathers are naturally red."

"Of course," I said, and beat a hasty retreat.

The billiard hall wasn't too crowded, and my crew staked out a table. Nlubglub chalked a cue stick. "Remember to compensate for the lighter Cygnoid gravity. And always keep one foot on the floor." They demonstrated, first stretching taller and sprouting a third arm to steady the cue.

"Are they allowed to do that?" Martian asked. "I should build a mechanical arm to even out the odds. Maybe with a little catapult."

Frink tried a shot, and sent the ball bouncing over the side of the table. A pink Cygnoid returned it, laughing.

"I'm a little out of practice," Frink said genially. "I play on my own planet, but the gravity's different here. Fancy a game? Maybe bet a few credits on it?"

"Sure," said the Cygnoid, and led Frink to another table.

The rest of us settled into the rhythm of the game. Around the third time we all lost to Nlubglub, a brightly dressed Plutonian walked in. "The *Turkey* crew, I was hoping I'd see you. How have you all been?"

Nlubglub eyed Skeeder, the only Plutonian in GUPPEAS. "Better, since you left our ship alone and moved to Captain Rossi's. What is that you're wearing?"

"The first officer is pretty relaxed about the uniform code when the captain's gone." Skeeder was probably wearing a GUPPEAS uniform; it was hard to tell underneath the red and silver sequins.

"'Relaxed' is not the word that comes to mind," Lola muttered.

"Wait," I said. "Why is Captain Rossi gone?"

"I don't know." Skeeder took down a cue stick and chalk. "She's taken off in the shuttle a few times. Sometimes she takes that Venusian reporter with her."

That got my attention. "Pietro?"

"Is he the one with the purple aura?" Skeeder took careful aim, peering over the stick, and missed hitting any of the other balls with the cue ball.

"Yes," I said. Richena must be using a normal shuttle, since her time-traveling one had been confiscated by GUPPEAS after the mission on Pluto. Unless she found a way to bring it back from the future? Forward from the past? "Where are they going?"

"Don't know. And she won't listen to any of my ideas for the wedding. You know she and Beau Dangere are getting married, right?"

"We've heard." Martian gave me a nervous glance, and tried to steer Skeeder to less dangerous topics. "About the shuttle trips—"

"I showed her my ideas for a dress—you know I designed the new GUPPEAS uniforms, right? But she wants to use one of her own designs. In only one color. Can you imagine anything so boring? Nothing but white."

"How long are they gone for?" To Skeeder's confused look, I added, "On the shuttle trips."

"I don't know, long enough for me to put decorative black mold on the bridge—you know, the kind Exalted Leader had dripping all over the palace? Captain Rossi didn't like it. She made me clean it all up." His antennae drooped. "Being on her ship is less fun than being on yours."

Across the room, I could see the pink Cygnoid handing over money and jewelry to Frink, who'd dropped the ruse of being an inexperienced player as soon as they made a wager.

At our table, Nlubglub made a trick shot that ended with the balls stacked in a neat pyramid.

"No fair," Skeeder huffed. "You didn't keep one foot on the floor."

Nlubglub sprouted a fist. "A Plutonian's accusing me of cheating?"

Skeeder raised his antennae defiantly, then shot the cue ball at Nlubglub's pyramid. The balls fell apart and bounced in every direction. When they came to rest, they spelled an obscene word in Plutonian. Skeeder set down the cue and marched away, antennae held high.

Shaking the cue stick ominously, Nlubglub stretched across the table—then suddenly contracted back into their normal shape, dropping the cue.

Pilar rushed to their side. "What's wrong? You're shaking."

"Having trouble with shape-shifting since the crash. I can manage an extra limb or two, but anything more than that is painful. The fall in the salon didn't help."

Pilar helped them up. "I told you to go easy on the shape-shifting. It'll heal naturally if you don't push it."

Frink returned to the table, wearing the Cygnoid's cloak.

"You cheated them out of the clothes on their back?" I asked.

"Technically, I only cheated them out of the money and rings. They didn't notice when I snagged the cloak."

The next afternoon, I walked to the chocolate shop and ordered chocolate mousse cake. It seemed wrong not to try each of their specialties at least once. I skimmed the news feed on my beepity-beeper, and there were a few videos showing fighting on Cassiopeia VII, but nothing to help me make sense of it. I tried not to focus on my worries for my parents, and for Randy.

I pulled out a book Pilar had given me: *StarMates: Finding Your Love Sign*. It recommended a Cygnoid astrology system for finding love. According to Cygnoid constellations, I was born under the sign of the flightless bird. My rising sign was a falling leaf, my falling sign was a flying fish, and my wandering-aimlessly-around sign was...I couldn't figure out the calculations involving the planet's four moons. I gave up.

A pair of Cygnoids glided past the window, looking lovingly at each other. Was this thing with Randy going anywhere? I couldn't tell. I dreamed of finding a man who sent my pulse skyrocketing, but maybe that was too much to ask, especially so soon.

"Glad I ran into you."

I looked up and my pulse skyrocketed.

Beau reached for the empty seat next to me, then paused. "Sorry, should have asked if you're saving this for someone."

Was I? It took me a second to remember.

"No, just getting my chocolate fix."

Beau ordered chocolate peanut butter pie. "I've been trying to come up with a new approach to convince the Cygnoids to change their plans. That first meeting didn't go too well."

"Not sure what we could have done differently." My fork drew swirls in the frosting on my cake. "Why didn't Richena come with us to meet with the Counselor?"

"Busy with wedding plans. Well, that and dealing with having a Plutonian in the crew. Skeeder wants to redesign the bridge in colors that can cause eye damage in most species."

"She could solve both problems and put Skeeder in charge of wedding plans."

Beau chuckled. "I'm trying to picture Skeeder's idea of a wedding gown. Maybe five hundred mismatched socks all stitched together."

"With a matching tux for you."

Maybe it was my imagination, but a hint of emotion flickered across his face. Regret, maybe.

I went for the easiest change of subject. "There has to be something the Counselor wants."

Beau scrunched his forehead, thinking. "Exalted Leader on Pluto wanted to control the fuelstone market. Dude Who Signs the Paychecks on Gemini XII wanted access to rare sports memorabilia. The Counselor mostly wants to talk down to people and feel in control, as far as I can tell. And the so-called Civilizer is serving pretty well for that."

I ground my teeth. "What about the other Cygnoids? How do they feel about all this?"

"The ones I've talked to are happy. They're convinced that they're saving the galaxy."

An incoming call pinged for him, and I glimpsed Richena's name. "Excuse me a minute." He stepped outside, but I caught snatches of the conversation through the open window. "I thought we were going to wait... No, of course I'm not having second thoughts... Come on, we're in the middle of this situation with the Cygnoids, and I could use your help with that..."

I tore my eyes away from the window and took another bite of cake. This was none of my business. What Beau and I had was over—technically, in this timeline, it had never happened—and I'd moved on.

"That's not funny, you know that I would never..."

I was not going to listen. I ordered more coffee. Quietly.

"No, I'm here at the chocolate shop with Captain Delane... What?... No... Why would you ask me that?... We were talking about the Counselor and what to do about the Civilizer."

A purple shadow loomed over me. "Janet, I should have known you'd be where the chocolate is."

I looked up to see Pietro, a slice of chocolate cheesecake in one hand and a milkshake in the other. I tried to keep my annoyance out of my voice. "Looks to me like we're both where the chocolate is."

Pietro set his food down and took over the seat next to me, elbowing Beau's plate aside. "Wasn't that dating show awesome? All the good parts were my idea. Wait until you get to the twist, where the couple goes on a date, but they're secretly being sabotaged by..."

He was still talking, but I was straining to hear Beau. No luck. I casually glanced out the window and saw him headed back inside.

Pietro was still nattering on. "And once the Counselor sees how good it is, I'm sure they'll let me work on the super-secret TV show."

Beau came up next to him. "What super-secret show?"

"If I knew that, it wouldn't be a secret, would it? But they've rerouted a lot of guards to the TV tree. Building. Building tree. Whatever. And the machinery they're bringing in doesn't look like camera or sound equipment. I tried to take a picture of it, and the guards went apoplectic, practically lost their feathers over it. Told me if I put anything in my column about it, they'd spread fake pictures of me wearing last year's fashions and I'd never be able to show my face again." Pietro shuddered. "Can you imagine? They'd make it look like I was wearing Neptunian water dancing shoes."

Beau and I looked at each other. I was pretty sure we were thinking the same thing. I said, "We should talk to GUPPEAS about this."

"Agreed. We need to figure out a plan."

Pietro looked confused. "Which part? The TV show or the water dancing shoes?"

Beau ignored him. "Richena's on her way over. Maybe we can figure something out."

I already had a plan, and it didn't involve Richena. "Oh, look at the time. I need to go." I scurried out.

After stopping by the ship for a quick favor from Frink, I strolled up to the guard at the front door of the TV building. "I'm here to meet with Grebe for the dating show. Are the rest of the participants here already?"

The guard squinted at me, confused. "They're not filming today."

"Grebe told me they were." I showed my beepity-beeper, with Frink's forged message that appeared to be from Grebe. "It's okay, I know where the studio is."

I couldn't find an elevator, or even stairs, but I found a door that led to the trunk of the tree that the building was constructed around. The trunk was as big around as the *Turkey*. The bark was rough enough that I was able to climb, with occasional scratches and a couple of scary slips, to the next floor. I followed a branch to the nearest door and was relieved to see this part of the building had a solid floor. Maybe they were used to aliens visiting, or maybe they had to accommodate the occasional Cygnoid with an injured wing.

I had no real plan other than to search for any signs of the weapon. I'd come at the end of the day, in hopes that not many people would be around. I'd been tempted to bring the crew with me, but that would have attracted attention, and I couldn't think of a plausible-sounding excuse for all of us to be there.

I listened at each door before cautiously opening it and peering around. One sound stage after another, some looking unused, others showing signs of recent activity. One looked like it had been the scene of a massive banana pudding fight. I eased that door shut and moved on.

Footsteps echoed around the corner. I looked around quickly for an escape route. Try the window, or the door next to me? The window probably led to a long drop. I yanked the door open to reveal a dark closet with a bunch of cloaks hanging. I squeezed inside and pulled the door shut.

One of the cloaks was moving.

I clamped a hand over my own mouth to keep from screaming. The Counselor's voice echoed in the hallway.

"We'll need an extra rotation of guards to protect the room with the Civilizer. I want patrols every thirty minutes."

"Very good, Counselor." Grebe's voice.

"And send a fruit basket to the Plutonians, so they know we're not holding any hard feelings."

"Hang on, I forgot my cloak."

I wriggled toward the back of the closet. There was movement again—someone was making sure the cloaks were between me and the door.

The door opened, and in the sudden light I could see that I was squeezed against Beau Dangere.

We both silently mouthed, *What are you doing here?*

"It's in here somewhere," came Grebe's voice. "When are you going to let the aliens know about the rest of the plan?"

"About turning each planet into a themed reality show?" The Counselor's voice was almost criminally cheerful. "We'll wait until they've all agreed to our proposal for peace under Cygnoid rule, no backsies. Although I'm rethinking the details. I like your idea for a dating show to assign mates for humans. But the loser should have to marry Pietro."

My life flashed before my eyes, with a soundtrack of "Here Comes the Bride."

Grebe squealed. "He'll like that."

"And speaking of Pietro, my new plan for Venusians is a show where they have to confront their deepest fears: falling from great heights, being exiled to a frozen planet, wrestling a giant space squid, that sort of thing."

"Pretty sure Pietro's greatest fear is the fashion police." Grebe chuckled obsequiously. "What about Jupiterans?"

"That's the best one. We can have gladiator games, a battle to the death, except Jupiterans are almost indestructible so they won't die. Probably."

"Here it is." Grebe pulled away a cloak, and I crouched down to avoid being seen. "They're a weird species. Not as weird as humans, though. Humans are always having wars and catastrophes and terrible sitcoms, and now they complain about how you go about making peace? It's a miracle they didn't nuke their entire planet for fun."

"Give it a few days," said the Counselor's voice.

"Ha! Good one." The door closed and we were in the dark again.

The Counselor's voice was still audible. "I meant, give it a few days and they'll see that our intervention is really in their best interests."

"Right. Of course. That's, um, what I meant too."

"And if not, we have a little surprise for them on the twelfth floor. Hey, why isn't my cloak flapping?"

"The little fan stopped working. What is it with technology today?"

The voices and footsteps faded, and I risked a whisper. "What are you doing here?"

Beau's mouth was right up against my ear. "Looking for clues about where they're hiding the weapon. You?"

"Same." I strained to hear through the door. "Think it's safe to go out yet?"

"Better wait a couple more minutes." Beau tried to shift positions, but there was no way we weren't going to be pushed against each other. His breath smelled like chocolate. "Sorry, trying not to squash you."

I was tempted to tell him I didn't mind. Instead I said, "That reality show idea is genius, in an evil way. It will keep creating humiliating moments that can be used against people with the Civilizer."

"Especially if they stick with the idea about a dating show. Think of all the ways a first date can turn out to be a disaster."

I could think of more than I cared to admit. "You could go for a long walk on the beach, only nobody warned you about the Plutonian chomperfish. Though that's still better than seeing Queelchu's last movie."

"I like her movies." Before I could answer, he added, "Wait, was her last movie the zombie romance on the planet of giant bunnies? You're right, that one was terrible. Maybe even worse than a first date where they ditched you in the restaurant and stole your wallet."

"Or when your date's idea of a good time is to search a TV studio, and you wind up hiding in a closet."

"That could have an upside."

I couldn't believe he'd said that. I was pretty sure he couldn't believe it either. There was a silence where I could hear both of our hearts pounding.

The door swung open, and someone swept the cloaks aside.

We both spoke at once. "Richena!"

9

Regelworms in Your Chocolate

Richena kept Beau's arm in a death grip as we crept down the hall, looking for the way up to the twelfth floor. "I haven't seen an elevator," I told them. "I came up the tree trunk."

"We got in through a window," Beau said, "but there has to be a freight elevator. Even an avian species wouldn't haul all that TV equipment up without one."

The floor was laid out in a maze, with bare branches near the giant trunk, and solid floors and walls further outward. The rooms were labeled for various reality shows, and the species that would apparently be subjected to them. "Death Duel (Jupiter)." "Real Fuel-stone Miners (Pluto)." "Build a Better Robot (Cassiopeia VII)."

We almost missed the freight elevator, which was unlabeled. We stepped inside and activated the control panel. "Twelfth floor," I said.

The elevator plunged down, much too fast.

"Stop," Richena hissed. "Stop. Stop!"

The elevator dropped a little further, then it jerked to a stop and the door opened. "Basement level," it said.

"Twelfth floor." Richena poked at the control panel. "Twelve. Twelve." The control panel coughed up a shower of sparks. One landed on my uniform sash, and I smacked it to keep it from catching fire.

Beau stepped off. "I don't think I want to try that again."

"Me either." I followed.

"Leave it to Jam-it to screw up the elevator." Richena stalked after us.

The basement was filled with camera equipment and machine parts, piled against the tree roots that snaked through the basement. Martian could probably have identified them, but the pieces all looked the same to me.

We found a staircase stretching upward for as far as we could see. I stifled a groan. "Want to give the elevator another try?"

Richena elbowed past me and marched up the stairs, setting a rapid pace. Beau followed. I took a deep breath, and climbed.

And climbed.

And climbed.

We were all dripping with sweat by the time we dragged ourselves onto the twelfth story. I sank down onto the floor, every muscle in my body aching. This was another area with a real floor and walls, and a confusing intersection of passages.

Richena drew in a ragged breath, trying to act as if she wasn't exhausted. "We should split up. Beau and I will take the left. Janet, you go right."

Beau leaned hard on the wall. "We should rest first."

"No time." She pulled him toward one side of the maze of hallways.

I staggered to my feet and down the hall to a nook with a water fountain shaped like a birdbath. The lukewarm water was a blessed relief, and I gulped some down and then splashed my face. The moment Richena and Beau turned the corner, I sank back down to the floor again. Despite the lighter-than-Earth gravity, my body felt too heavy to lift. Maybe I would sit under the birdbath forever and never move again. That seemed like a good career choice.

A few minutes slipped by. I heard Richena's voice: "This one's for a cooking show."

I needed to get to work on searching for the Civilizer, or this whole effort was pointless. I needed to save the galaxy. More immediately, I needed another drink of water. But nothing could convince my body to do anything except sit there.

"Run!"

Beau and Richena raced past me at top speed, neither registering my presence.

Two Vegans came barreling past, teeth snapping.

One of the Vegans noticed me, stopped, and turned. It looked hungry. And it was between me and the stairs.

I sprang to my feet and ran the other way, faster than I'd ever moved in my life. I turned a corner and found myself facing a dead end. On my right was a double door with a bright pink warning label: "Restricted Area." On my left, the floor gave way to a ragged web of branches around the tree trunk. Heavy footsteps were catching up behind me.

I tried the door. Locked.

Trusting this planet's lighter gravity, I jumped to a branch a few feet down. I steadied myself against the trunk, and jumped again. Down and down, one branch to the next. Almost to the ground floor. I might make it, if I didn't look up.

I looked up.

The Vegan was peering down at me from a long way above, through an open spot in the leaves. It took aim, and jumped all the way down to my branch. The branch gave a loud crack, then broke off and tumbled toward the ground—Vegan, me, and all.

We landed in a heap in the building lobby. The Vegan moaned and sat up. I struggled to my feet and fled out the emergency exit, setting off an alarm that wailed like a Saturnian lizard-cow. I looked back, hoping the Vegan wasn't following.

It was following, teeth bared in anticipation.

We raced down the dark street. Why didn't I have a weapon? What had possessed me to join a peace organization, only to end my life as an appetizer for a dentally over-endowed alien?

The shops were closed, but the nearest door opened to my shove. I grabbed the first throwable item, a heavy pot. I turned, aimed, and gave the Vegan a face full of...

...chocolate?

The Vegan stopped and looked at me, chocolate sauce dripping down its face. "Wow." It picked up the pot from the floor and took another taste. "This is delicious. What is it?"

It took a moment to find my voice. "It's called chocolate. It's from Earth."

"This is what Earthlings taste like?"

"No." I took a step back. "It's from a bean." I glanced around the chocolate shop and saw a tray of brownies. "There's more over there."

The Vegan descended on the brownies with gusto, and I tried to sneak out the back door.

My beepity-beeper went off, almost as loudly as the alarm earlier. I reached for it, hit the wrong button, and heard Beau's voice fill the room. "Janet, are you okay? Are you safe?"

The Vegan moved on to the fridge, paying no attention to me.

"Fine," I told Beau. "And I've figured out the key to that diplomatic mission GUPPEAS was planning to send to Vega."

Beau called early the next morning. "Can we talk in person? It's important."

"Of course." My heart was already doing gymnastics, wondering what he wanted.

"Richena and I will be right over."

They arrived halfway through my first cup of coffee. I left it unfinished, which is always a mistake when I'm trying to wake up, and escorted them to the view room. Beau shot an awkward glance at Richena, cleared his throat, and finally looked back at me. "There's something we need to ask you about."

"About getting to the weapon? I had a couple of ideas, but we're going to need more information."

"No, not about that." Beau seemed strangely nervous, fingers tapping on the viewscreen. "It's a personal matter."

Richena gave an ingratiating smile. "You know Beau and I are getting married."

"Sure," I said. I wanted to grab Beau and shake him, tell him this was all wrong for him. If only there was a way to make him believe it.

The silence stretched on, and I finally said, "Congratulations."

Beau cleared his throat again. "There's one problem. We can't get anyone to perform the ceremony."

"The local magistrates won't do it because we're not citizens," Richena added. "The Counselor could do it, but he doesn't believe in people choosing their own mates, unless it's on a reality show with fifty potential spouses to choose from, and an option for polygamy."

Behind her on the viewscreen, Cygnoids were flying all around the spaceport, several wearing the red cloaks that identified them as security.

"There's a loophole." Beau leaned toward me. "A spaceship captain can perform the ceremony on their ship."

My under-caffeinated mind was moving at half speed. There were lots of ships here, lots of captains. "That shouldn't be a problem."

"See?" Beau beamed at Richena. "I told you she'd help us."

"Wait, what?"

"We need you to perform the wedding." Richena's voice bit off the end of the last word, as if she was trying to keep from adding *you idiot.*

On the viewscreen, two of the Cygnoid security officers crashed into each other.

I scrambled for an excuse. "I've never performed a wedding. I'd totally screw it up."

"There's no technology involved." Beau attempted a smile. "You'll be fine."

The computer struck up a soft rendition of "Here Comes the Bride." I drew a breath between gritted teeth. "And there's barely any room on the *Turkey*. And, Beau, don't you want your sister Bonbon there, and your brother Mal, and the rest of your family?"

"My siblings are on seven different planets right now. If we wait to get all of them together, there's never going to be a wedding." A realization hit him. "When did I tell you about my sister Bonbon?"

In the other timeline. "I don't know, I'm sure you mentioned her. Or maybe Richena mentioned her. Anyway—"

"Who does your hair?" Richena interrupted. "I was going to try that Cygnoid salon, but their wait list is months long, and they said they didn't know what to do with, I quote, those extra-fine feathers."

"Zeeko does everyone's hair on the ship." Although I had a hard time picturing Richena with anything except the immovable knot perched on top of her head.

"I finished making my dress, so that's taken care of, and Beau already has a tux. Maybe get something from the botanical garden for decoration."

"All we have to do is keep your pilot away from the rings," Beau added.

"Great, it's all settled." Richena pulled Beau toward the door. "Thanks, Janet, you're a true friend."

"But—"

The Counselor's voice boomed over the intercom. "We are broadcasting this on all channels. Someone tried to break in and access the Civilizer last night. We are very disappointed in you. Security is currently searching for the culprit, and when we find them, they need to be taught a lesson. Perhaps we should use them as test subjects for the next upgrade of the Civilizer."

I turned, but Richena and Beau were already gone.

I returned to the bridge and sank into my chair. Pilar eyed me curiously. "Everything all right, Captain?"

Besides the Counselor making threats of mayhem? "Beau and Richena want to get married on the *Turkey*."

Frink looked up with interest. "Where will they be storing the wedding presents?"

"Oh, shut up," Lola said. "This is terrible. The captain's going to be miserable, and she's going to make all of us miserable."

Zeeko blinked slowly. "Can I do their hair?"

"Nobody's doing hair. Or stealing wedding presents. A *Turkey* wedding is not happening." After a few more piano notes, I added, "Computer, if you don't stop that music, I'm replacing you with an abacus."

Martian scrutinized my face. "If the wedding's not happening, then why do you look like you found regelworms in your chocolate?"

"Beau and Richena think it is happening. I'll straighten it out. I'll send a message right now, and tell them I can't do it because…uh, because…"

"You don't have to give a reason," Pilar said. "A reason gives them something to argue against. Tell them you can't do it, and don't budge from that."

"Good advice," I said. "I'll do that before this has a chance to go any further."

"I still get to steal the wedding presents, right?" Frink gave me a hopeful look.

"No." I thought for a moment. "Yes. If you can find them, knock yourself out."

I went to my quarters and composed a message to Beau.

I'm honored that you asked me to officiate at your wedding. But I can't do it. I'm sorry, and I hope you understand.

I sent the message, then saw an incoming one from my mother.

We're about to land on Cassiopeia VII. By the way, did you see Pietro's latest column? If I didn't know any better, I'd think he wanted you back. Your brother said you were trying online dating, but I can never tell when he's joking. Though I'm sure there are plenty of nice young men who would be happy to date an up-and-coming spaceship captain. The communication equipment has been iffy since we got here, but we'll write when we can.

Cassiopeia VII. My parents were about to land in a war zone, and I was light-years away and couldn't do anything about it. My hands were shaking so hard, I couldn't read the screen. I set the beepity-beeper on my desk.

There were two more incoming messages. One was from Vertin Bogler at GUPPEAS, asking why someone had signed the *Turkey* up for an extended warranty. *Doesn't everyone in the universe know that's a scam?*

I saved the message from Randy for last. *Want to tour the botani-*

cal garden with me? It's supposed to be amazing.

I thought about Beau, and how close he'd been to me in the closet.

This had to stop. Beau was off-limits, Randy was nice, I needed to cheer myself up, and I'd never toured a botanical garden before. I'd never given a moment's thought to the existence of botanical gardens. Time to try something new.

Sounds like fun. Tomorrow?

10

YLILACSOP

The garden turned out to be gorgeous, filled with colorful flowers and trees in shapes I'd never seen before. There were line-dancing hedges, inside-out trees, and Neptunian flowers with a scent so strong that it was illegal to pilot a spaceship for six hours after smelling them. Randy gravitated toward the Earth section, checking out the jasmine and palm trees. I had to warn him about touching the poison ivy.

"Earth sounds like an interesting place." Randy stopped to examine a weeping willow. "I've been reading Earth literature, but I don't understand it very well."

"Probably better than I'd understand literature from your planet." It was flattering that he'd been interested enough to research my planet. I'd tried to learn more about his, but very little information was available. "What have you been reading?"

"*Romeo and Juliet.* This is supposed to be the ultimate Earthling romance? I didn't care for the ending."

"Yeah, killing off the characters is not a typical love-story ending. The preferred one is 'happily ever after.'"

"That's a relief." A shrieking shrub let out a wail from somewhere further down the path, and he had to wait for it to finish before he continued. "Also, the plot had an incredible number of coincidences, and several communication problems that could have been cleared up with a cell phone."

"It's famous because of the poetic language. Like the part about how a rose by any other name would smell as sweet."

Randy bent to sniff a rose, frowning as he poked a finger on the thorns. "I liked the poetry, but why did it say they were 'star-crossed'? Earth only has one star, right? Sol."

"It's an expression." I hoped his language had room for metaphors. "Some Earthlings believe the stars determine our fate. Star-crossed means unlucky. A star-crossed couple is one that's not meant to be."

"Oh. I thought it was related to having a double sun, like this planet. Which would make everyone here star-crossed, I guess."

"It's starting to feel star-crossed. Nothing's gone right since I've been in the Pelican Nebula."

"Uh..."

"Except for meeting you, obviously." I wanted to smack myself, which made me feel more star-crossed than ever. I scrambled for a change of subject. "What kind of stories do you like?"

His forehead crinkled. "Popular literature forms on my planet are different. They're written in trinary code, and you have to complete the mathematical formula to separate it into paragraphs. Also, some of the languages don't have nouns."

I heard a ping, announcing a news alert. I ignored it. "How can it not have nouns? We're all nouns."

"The same way your language doesn't have *gliknunks*. At least one Cygnoid language doesn't have adjectives, and I can think of lots of adjectives that apply to them."

"True."

"Anyway, we also have the concept of loves that are fated to be, or not. There's a story about two robots in love, but they keep causing each other's magnetic field to reverse, so they can never be together. Cassiopeian stories are structured like a flowchart, or a decision tree, and you have to get through the wrong ones so you can find the right one."

A flowchart? I tried to picture that. "It would be simpler if you could start with the right one."

We stopped in front of a Lyran harp plant, its vines vibrating musically in the breeze. Randy smiled. "But you learn from each of the wrong ones. For instance, from Pietro you learned not to date a guy who spends all his time writing about himself."

"It's still better than when he writes about me." I stopped myself. Complaining about exes was not a great way to impress a date, even if Randy was the one who'd brought it up. "I do have one other ex who was really nice. It didn't work out because...I don't know, it's complicated. What about you?"

"Nobody too serious. I'm still getting the hang of dating."

"Isn't everyone?" An idea occurred to me. "What was that thing you said our language doesn't have?"

"*Gliknunks*. Why?"

"My brother invented a universal translator, and he put a simplified version in my beepity-beeper." I got it out and turned on the translator function.

A murmur of voices rose from the device.

This garden was such a good idea. I love that it brings the fauna here so we can look at them.

So many different shapes and colors, and the noises they make, fascinating.

And the smells, don't forget the smells.

Check out the small one there; it's turning red.

Randy and I looked at each other. He found his voice first. "Are the plants talking about us?"

Are the fauna eavesdropping on us? That is so rude.

"Sorry about that," I said to any plants that might be listening. "I'll turn the translator off." I switched it off and started to put the beepity-beeper away, but it clunked with a call from the ship. "I have to take this."

I stepped away from Randy and picked up the call. Lola's face filled my screen, and the dark red of her aura told me that it wasn't good news. "Morning, Captain. Have you been watching the news?"

"Uh, no, I'm on a date right now."

Frink's cheery voice broke in from the background. "I told you so!"

Lola continued, "Thought you'd want to know that Richena Rossi was caught on the security camera at the Cygnoid TV building last night. She was seen with two unidentified companions."

"Unidentified?"

"Yeah. Lucky for them, whoever they were. Richena was the only one hit by the Civilizer. They're running the footage on every news channel."

Somewhere past the next grove of trees, I heard Randy's voice: "Check this one out; it's from Venus."

My eyes were still on the beepity-beeper, where Lola's face was replaced by footage of Richena writhing around on the floor, scream-ing and moaning. I heard something that sounded like my name, but it was hard to hear clearly. Here in the garden I heard another shrieking shrub, nearby this time. "What did she say?"

"I had Zeeko listen to it, and according to his giant cone-ears, Richena said, 'Not Janet Delane! Get her out of my face!'"

"I'm part of her most embarrassing moment?" I might have enjoyed that thought a little too much.

"Sounds like it. Did you make her floatcar tie itself in a knot?"

"No, I think it was about...something else." I didn't want to bring up Beau when I was here with Randy. "We need to figure out how to get to the Civilizer, before anyone else gets hurt. I'll be back soon." I ended the call and looked around. "Randy?"

Another shriek filled the air. It didn't sound like a shrub. It sounded like Randy.

I ran in the direction that I'd last heard his voice. As I emerged from a clump of trees, I nearly plowed into a giant Venus flytrap with a pair of legs sticking out of its trap.

I reached for my weapon.

I didn't have a weapon. I worked for a peace organization.

I turned the translator back on. "Put my friend down, or I'll shoot you with my laser!"

The plant spat Randy out. "That tastes disgusting," it said. "What species are you?"

"Human," I said automatically, though it presumably meant

Randy.

"I am never touching another human again," the plant said. According to a nearby warning sign, it was a true Venus flytrap, not the tiny kind we see on Earth. "Your species tastes gross."

"Good to know," I said. "You don't want Cassiopeians either. We taste the same."

"I'm gonna puke up all my pollen."

I helped a dazed Randy to his feet and led him toward the exit.

"Thanks," he said. "It took me by surprise."

"Let's get out of here."

He clutched his stomach, looking ill. "Let's."

Why did I smell smoke again?

After returning to the ship, I spent the afternoon in the relative normalcy of breaking up squabbles between crew members. Then came an unexpected message.

"Requesting permission for entry." Skeeder Boredan's voice.

I looked around to make sure Nlubglub wasn't on the bridge. Getting them in the same room with a Plutonian was never a good idea. "Permission granted."

Skeeder entered the bridge a moment later, lugging a harp plant like the one I'd seen at the botanical garden with Randy. "Where do you want this?"

"What do you mean?"

Skeeder set the pot down so hard, the bridge quivered. He had augmented his eight-colored GUPPEAS uniform with an assortment of tassels and glittery patches. "I have more plants outside. Can you help me carry them in?"

I tried not to get distracted by a patch on his shoulder, which was either purple or orange depending on which way the light hit it. "Skeeder, why are you bringing plants onto my ship?"

"Wedding decorations. Captain Rossi said to bring them from the botanical garden." After a moment, he added, "Was I supposed to ask the gardeners first?"

I looked at Skeeder. "When is this wedding supposed to be?"

"Sixteen hundred hours."

"What day?"

His antennae quivered in surprise. "Today."

"I told them I can't do the wedding." I pulled out my beepity-beeper, and saw a message from Beau.

Thanks for agreeing to do this. It means a lot to Richena and me.

I checked my outgoing messages, and saw what I'd sent to him earlier.

I'm honored that you asked me to officiate at your wedding. The rest of the message had never sent. It was followed by a second text I'd apparently sent to both Beau and Randy: *Sounds like fun. Tomorrow?*

"Computer, what did you do to me?"

The computer giggled. "Wasn't me. You must have messed up the communication equipment."

Heavy steps echoed in the corridor. I walked out to find Frink carrying a massive bush with flowers in a dozen colors. "There's a whole bunch of nice-looking plants outside. I'm going to put this in my quarters."

"It should go over there." Skeeder pointed next to my chair. "Are the caterers here yet?"

"You." Frink put the bush down and glared at Skeeder. "Last time you were here, you stole all our socks." Frink took it personally, since the whole crew had blamed him for the sock thefts.

"That's not true. I left you one from every pair. And I made a really fetching robe out of them, but of course it wasn't formal enough to wear to a wedding."

"There isn't supposed to be a wedding." My voice was drowned out by the sound of the caterers tromping up the ramp, with a cart full of Cygnoid delicacies. I eyed a gorgeous wedding cake decorated in frills of frosting. "Any chance that's chocolate?"

"Nah, Captain Rossi doesn't like chocolate." Skeeder reached toward the cake, and had his hand slapped away by a Cygnoid caterer.

"I don't understand her either."

My bridge was filling up with plants and members of Richena's crew. The caterers asked directions to the mess hall and disappeared. And that purple glow couldn't mean what I thought it meant.

It did. It was Pietro's aura, shining brightly as he came up the ramp with a fancy camera.

"This is all wrong," I said weakly.

"Of course it is." Skeeder fussed with the arrangement of blossoms. "Have you seen the dress she's wearing? I tried to help her out with it, but she wouldn't listen to any of my suggestions."

I looked again at Skeeder's outfit, which could have been designed by sentient hallucinogenic mushrooms. "How surprising. But I never agreed to—"

"Janet." Beau's voice rose over the crowd, and they parted to make way for him and Richena. He was in a tuxedo, and she was in uniform with a large garment bag over her arm. Beau clasped my hand in both of his. "Thank you again for doing this."

Richena looked recovered from her ordeal with the Civilizer, and she attempted a smile at me. "You're putting on a dress uniform, right?"

"Um, sure."

"There's one thing." Beau looked like he'd rather be in a Plutonian fuelstone mine. "The ring seems to have disappeared again."

"Oh, come on." Frink used his smoothest conman voice. "You left it in an outside pocket. It was like you wanted me to take it."

"Could be a subconscious thing," Pilar added helpfully.

Richena grabbed at Frink. He tried to dodge, but he was used to evading Lola and forgot that not everyone was left-handed. He moved straight into her grip, and she twisted his arm around his back.

"Go get the ring and hand it over," Richena said pleasantly, "or I'll rip your face off and feed it to the Vegans."

Frink stammered something that might have been a yes, and headed for the lift.

"Glad we got that settled," Richena said. "Where do I go to get changed?"

Lola pointed. "Left at the end of that hallway, then second door on the right."

After Richena left, I murmured, "The shuttle bay?"

Lola leaned in to answer, "Martian's ice-rink thingy is still in there. We were practicing curling earlier."

The bridge was crammed: my crew, Richena's crew, and people I'd never seen before. The plants were everywhere, with crepe paper hearts and bells hanging from their branches. I escaped to my quarters and put on a dress uniform. It was possibly the only thing worse than what Skeeder was wearing. Ten colors? I picked up my beepity-beeper and saw a message from Martian.

You should get back down here. Nlubglub and Skeeder got in an argument over who dropped a plant on whose foot. Lola was trying to keep things under control, but then she tried to slug Pietro. I missed exactly why.

I sighed and looked in the mirror, making one last adjustment to the dress uniform hat, which didn't match the shirt, which didn't match the pants, boots, or sash. I made my way to the bridge, and squeezed past a few of Richena's crew members.

As I took my place at the front of the room, the harp plant began playing the familiar strains of "Here Comes the Bride." The computer added a piano accompaniment. Richena slowly marched up the aisle, soaking up the admiration from everyone around her. I had to admit the dress was a work of art, dazzling crystals covering silk and lace, with a train that extended for yards behind her. A delicate veil was pinned to the waves of perfectly styled auburn hair swirling around her face, which was decidedly scowling.

It was subtle, but I realized she was walking slowly because she was limping. From the look she shot at Lola, I guessed things hadn't gone well in the ice-covered shuttle bay. Richena reached the front of the room and joined hands with Beau, who looked…

…miserable.

Was I projecting my own feelings onto Beau? A groom supposed to look happy. I could understand a serious expression for such an important moment, but his eyes should be shining with joy, right? Beau looked like he'd just remembered he'd left the iron on.

Everyone was watching me, waiting for me to begin.

"Dearly beloved." I looked directly at Beau.

Richena gave me a glare that could have sliced the diamond ring in half.

I started again. "Dearly beloved, we are gathered here today to unite this man and this woman in holy misery. Matrimony. What do we mean by 'holy matrimony'?" I strained to remember what I'd read about marriage in *The Space-Faring Moron's Guide to Common Science Fiction Plot Devices*. "On Pluto, marriages are celebrated by the couple stacking fish on each other's heads. At Ursan weddings, the couple must find and steal a coin hidden in each other's clothes, to symbolize stealing each other's hearts. A Jupiteran marriage may have as many as a hundred participants, though eight to twenty are more common. Some time-travelers divorce before the wedding. And in the Spider Nebula, the female devours—"

Richena cranked the glare up to a level that could split a planet in half.

"If anyone has a reason why this marriage should not take place, speak now or forever hold your peace." I risked another look at Beau.

There was a moment of silence.

This is completely ridiculous. What are we doing here?

Richena looked around wildly. "Who said that?"

I think we're supposed to watch them, like in the garden.

I looked at the flowering shrub. "Did somebody leave the universal translator on? Because I think that was the plants." At least there was no Venus flytrap this time.

Are the fauna eavesdropping on us again? So rude. We'd never do that to them.

Except when that one Plutonian—what was its name? Something Leader?—wouldn't stop talking about how they'd come up with a better weapon to counter the Cygnoid one.

And they said tonight was the time for the attack. Fauna have such strange behavior. Why can't they get along?

Plutonians are like weeds; they don't get along with anyone.

Nlubglub sprang to their feet. "An attack tonight? We have to stop them."

"Right. Everybody out." Lola herded the guests toward the door. "Computer, red alert."

There was a brief silence.

I looked at the computer with irritation. "Aren't you supposed to make an alarm noise?"

"I was never programmed for one."

"Make one up." Lola's aura darkened. "Or I'll smack you."

A deafening alarm filled the room, and the lights blinked red.

"Sorry about this," I told Beau and Richena. "I guess the wedding will have to wait?"

"Of course," Beau said quickly.

"Of course not," Richena said simultaneously.

They looked at each other. Richena was fuming. "You can't be serious."

Beau's voice was at his most reasonable. "There's going to be an attack. You and Janet are captains in the GUPPEAS fleet. It's our responsibility to stop this."

"And these aren't exactly dream wedding circumstances." I had to raise my voice over the alarm.

Richena hiked up her skirt, turned, and flounced toward the door, tossing Beau's ring over her shoulder as she left. Frink made a spectacular dive, but Beau still caught it first.

Pilar stayed behind to deal with the wedding guests, and the rest of my crew and I piled into Beau's floatcar. "What's our plan?" he asked.

Everyone looked at me.

I tried to think. "Start with rational persuasion, and work our way up to gently tapping their weapon with a sledgehammer?"

Nlubglub's expression suggested they were unimpressed. "Let's grab the Plutonians, dump them in front of the Counselor, and watch the Cygnoids use their weapon again."

I shook my head. "Nlubglub."

"So that we can, you know, study the Cygnoid weapon. In the interests of interplanetary peace."

"Can we kidnap Adequate Leader?" Frink sounded chipper. "It worked out pretty well last time we did a kidnapping."

Frink's idea of "worked out pretty well" differed a bit from mine. Pluto's former leader had nearly vaporized us. "We are not doing kidnappings. We're a peace organization. But if you can figure out a way to steal their weapon, let me know."

"Let you know before I steal it, or after?"

I aimed a pointed look at his hand, which was reaching for Beau's pocket. "Before."

We heard the Plutonian ship before we saw it. A strange grinding, roaring, scratching noise, worse than the alarms we'd heard on the *Turkey*, more like a diabolical mechanical creature screaming in agony. Martian sent us a group text: *A noise-torture weapon?*

By the time Beau stopped the floatcar in front of the berth where the Plutonian ship was docked, Zeeko was doubled over with his hands shielding his oversized ears. I typed *stay here* on my beepity-beeper, and held the screen in front of his face until he nodded.

The ship's ramp was down and the hatch left open. We tried hailing them first, but with no answer, we walked in.

The bridge of the ship was filled with Plutonians, some in uniform and some in their nightclothes. Adequate Leader was in a purple polka-dotted nightshirt, with his antennae in curlers. All of them were clutching their ears as Zeeko had been doing. Every spare nook and cranny was filled with noisy machinery, all of it running at once: music players, kitchen mixers, chainsaws, a curling-stone polisher, a video of a Neptunian croakbird screaming contest, and something that looked like a detached floatcar engine.

I turned off the nearest machines, one at a time, but there were so many that it wasn't making an appreciable dent in the sound. Lola punched a food processor, spattering its contents all over the wall. Adequate Leader yelled at us, or at least it looked like he did.

Martian elbowed aside the Plutonian at the main computer

station, and got the computer to cut all the noise at once. It took a minute to stop the ringing in my ears.

Adequate Leader looked around at his crew. "Everyone all right?"

A crew woman moaned. "It's still there."

"Go to sick bay. And take a leaf blower with you." As the lift door closed behind her, I heard the leaf blower turn on.

Now that my head was clearing, I noticed a machine at the front of the bridge, shaped like a megaphone, but the size of a floatcar. Plutonian letters on the side spelled out "Ylilacsop."

Beau looked from the machine to Adequate Leader. "What is this?"

"It was supposed to save us." Adequate Leader's voice rasped, as if he'd been screaming for hours. He pulled a chair and sat with his head in his hands.

"Save you?" Beau gestured for him to continue.

"From the Cygnoids and their stupid weapon. This was our best chance. The Ylilacsop. But it backfired."

My eyes strayed back to the name inscribed on the side of the machine. It seemed familiar, and I wasn't sure why but I needed to push that thought out of my mind. "Backfired how?"

One of the other Plutonians looked up, her face a shattered plate of misery. "It's a simple concept. It gets a song stuck in your head. But instead of broadcasting to the Cygnoids, it got into our ship's sound system. Now the song's stuck in all of our heads too, and we can't get rid of it."

"Oh no," I said. "Whatever you do, don't say the name of the song."

"We tried *Baby Space Squid* and *You've Made the Down Payment, But You Haven't Signed the Mortgage on My Heart*. Those go away on their own, eventually. But we found the one tune that rattles around in your head and won't leave. We've been running chainsaws and jackhammers, trying to drown out the melody."

Beau looked at the weapon's name again, and blanched. "That song? Please, nobody say the name."

"There has to be a way to get rid of it," Adequate Leader moaned.

Zeeko wandered in. "Ylilacsop," he read aloud. "Hey, is that short for—"

"Don't!" we all yelled.

"Your Love Is Like a Cold Slice of Pizza?"

I clutched my temples as the familiar tune pounded its way inside my head.

Your love is like a cold slice of pizza,
Warmed over twice. (Twice!)
The anchovies are starting to sme-ell,
And the smell ain't nice. (Nice!)

I hated everything about that song. The distinctive "bum-pa-dum, bum-pa-dum" background vocals. The way it turned "smell" into a two-syllable word. The fact that it made me think about anchovies. But mostly I hated the catchy, bouncy tune that wouldn't stop.

The to-matoes are rotting away,
The red peppers have turned to gray.
Your love is like a cold slice of pizza
Warmed over tw—

Beau had his hands over his ears. "Make it stop!"

Zeeko blinked his fried-egg eyes. "Make what stop?" There was no way to explain to him that the song was as loud in my head as if it really had been playing. I'd heard it at a Green Pickles concert in high school, and it had banged around in my head for days.

So put on your coat (oo-woo-woo)
And go to the store (oo-woo-woo)
And get me a fresh pizza once more...

I called Pilar, raising my voice unnecessarily. "Is there a cure for earworm?"

"The Orion kind?"

"The musical kind."

"Recite alien alphabets backward, loud enough to drown the noise out. And whatever you do, don't tell me what the song was." She disconnected quickly.

I started with the Jupiteran alphabet, all 387 letters. Jupiterans were the only ones who always beat me at Scrabble. The rest of the crew recited a cacophony of Ursan, Saturnian, Venusian, and more. After a moment, I noticed that Beau was also doing the Jupiteran alphabet.

Beau grinned at me.

The song went away.

It was as good as a kiss.

11

Space Platypus

Beau dropped us back at the *Turkey*. My crew disappeared into the ship, one after the other, until only Beau and I were left. I noticed a tattered copy of *U, Robot* sitting in the cup holder. "Is that book any good?" I still needed to steal my copy back from Frink.

"No idea. It's Richena's." His voice was edged with exhaustion. "I'd better go try to talk things out with her."

"I'm sure she'll understand." I kept my voice bright, buoyed by the fact that the wedding hadn't happened—and for reasons not totally related to my incompetence as an officiant. "She must be an understanding person. Otherwise, marrying her would seem like a big horrible mistake, and you've never felt that way, right?"

"Right." Beau gave me a thin attempt at a smile.

I climbed out of the floatcar. "Are you doing okay?" Then, fearing I'd overstepped, I hastily added, "I mean, is that song out of your head now?"

"I think so." He didn't seem in a hurry to leave. "Janet, do you ever get the feeling that everything around you is wrong? Like you've been, I don't know, dropped into the wrong universe?"

I chose my words carefully. "Or the wrong timeline?"

His face lit up. "Exactly like that. Like the past got messed up, and now everything's spinning out of control, and you keep feeling this isn't how things were meant to be."

"You've always struck me as someone who can trust his feelings."

The memory burned across my mind like a comet: Beau and I practicing curling on the frozen river, green moons shining overhead, while we told each other our secrets. Could he see it now in my face?

"Sometimes I have these memories, except they can't be memories, because they couldn't have happened." Something in his eyes made me think I was part of those memories. "Janet…"

His beepity-beeper rang with a message. He glanced at it, and I knew without looking that it was Richena.

"I have to go." He shut the floatcar door and sped off.

On the bridge, Pilar was pulling down wedding decorations. "I had Skeeder take the plants back outside, and sent the caterers home. Lola wanted the crepe paper hearts to use for target practice. And I told all the guests to take the wedding presents with them."

I glanced over at Frink, who was at his station. He didn't seem to be paying attention.

"That's one disaster out of the way," I said. "But we still have the real disaster to deal with. How are we going to get to the Cygnoid weapon?"

"Preferably before the Plutonians have another genius idea," Nlubglub added. "It would help if we could tap into the guard schedules for that building."

"Leave that to me." Frink pulled up a page on his beepity-beeper. "One of the Cygnoid guards answered my ad on LuckyStar."

Zeeko called. "Captain? I'm in the shuttle bay, and there's a plant here."

"I thought Skeeder was supposed to take them all away."

"He tried. I think you'd better come down here."

I walked down to the shuttle bay, still sorting through alien alphabets in my head in case the song came back. I would have to give Skeeder a piece of my mind about bringing all these plants and other things onto my ship for a wedding that I'd never agreed to be part of.

The shuttle bay door opened to the sound of screaming. Skeeder was being used as the rope in a tug-of-war between Zeeko and the Venus flytrap. Skeeder's head and one arm were in the plant's mouth, and Zeeko was trying to pull him out by the legs.

I turned the translator on. "Drop him right now!"

Zeeko and the plant simultaneously dropped Skeeder onto the floor. He looked up and wailed, "You ruined my outfit."

The flytrap swiveled toward me, and I'm pretty sure it snarled. "You again? What are you doing here?"

"This is my ship. What are you doing here?"

"How should I know? I was in the garden, taking a nap, and when I woke up I was here in a pot. How would you like to wake up in a pot?"

"I'll call the Cygnoid authorities and have you taken back to the garden. Meantime, no eating people on my ship." I looked around at the crumpled remains of wedding decorations. "Remember, we have terrible taste."

When Zeeko and I returned to the bridge, the crew members were all there, and Frink was deep in a conversation over his beepity-beeper. "How do you feel about really bad comedy shows? ... Or going crater jumping? ... Hurling? I thought you said *curling.*"

I shot a look at him. "Could you set up your date somewhere else?"

Without interrupting the conversation, Frink sent a text that appeared in the air in front of me: *She's a Cygnoid guard. Martian's tracking her communicator through mine. She's on duty, so as long as she keeps talking we can create a map of the guard's rounds.*

"Right. Carry on." I sank into my chair and leaned back. I noticed an object dangling from the fire sprinkler. "What's that?"

Lola glanced up. "Pietro's camera. Must have flown there when I slugged him." She shrugged. "Shouldn't have asked me nosy questions about what crime I committed that got me into GUPPEAS."

"I'll get it." Nlubglub stretched a limb to the ceiling, but when they grabbed the camera, they started shaking. The camera dropped into my lap.

Pilar hurried to Nlubglub's side. "I told you not to overdo the shape-shifting."

"It's a reflex, growing another limb any time I need one." Nlubglub morphed back into their usual shape of a rubber ball with legs.

"Let's see what I can do for those tremors." Pilar bent to examine them.

I looked down at the camera. The last picture saved was one of me at the wedding, in that horrendous dress uniform. The shot was framed in a way that surrounded me with the hearts-and-flowers decorations. The effect was almost romantic. Annoyed, I erased the picture, then flipped through the next few. "This looks like the inside of the TV building. And is that...?"

Lola looked over my shoulder. "A hidden route directly to the restricted area."

I looked around the bridge. Pilar was escorting Nlubglub toward sick bay. Frink was sweet-talking the Cygnoid guard while Martian tracked the call. Lola went back to practicing martial arts, her kicks stopping a centimeter short of Zeeko's face. Zeeko looked unbothered.

"We have a lot of skills in this crew," I observed.

"I can do hair," Zeeko said, "and train lizards to reenact famous movie scenes. I can even make it look like the lizards have hair."

"I'm not sure that gets us any closer to the Civilizer."

"I also make light sculptures."

The crew and I waited until both suns had set before we piled into the floatcar. Frink flew us to the TV building and landed on the roof. We got out and peered over the sides of the building, but saw only trees and dark storefronts. All quiet.

I checked out the trapdoor entrance. "Martian, can you get the alarm?"

Martian frowned over one of his homemade devices. "The alarm is…" He double checked his readings. "…already off."

Frink reached for the handle, and the door opened before he got out his lockpicks.

I squinted down into the darkness. "This feels too easy." My flashlight showed an indoor tree limb leading to a floor of branches: uneven, but solid. We shimmied down, one at a time.

Nlubglub pulled up a screen on their beepity-beeper. "According to the guards' schedule, they should be at the other end of the building. The restricted area is this way." They pointed.

When we reached the door, Frink went to work disarming the lock. He chuckled with pleasure as the door slid open and we stepped inside.

Smack into Adequate Leader and a half dozen Plutonians armed with lasers.

"What are you doing here?" said several voices simultaneously.

Now I made sense of the disabled alarm and the unlocked door. "You have a cloaked ship on the roof, right?"

"Of course," Adequate Leader said. "We should have the Civilizer." His antennae waggled toward the far end of the room. The room was enormous, bigger than our shuttle bay, but the Civilizer was surprisingly small, about the size of a curling stone. There was a catwalk around the edges of the room for us to stand on, and the rest of the floor was a tangle of branches that didn't look terribly sturdy. The Civilizer lay in a nest, surrounded by an intricate network of laser beams that extended a few meters around it.

Adequate Leader was still talking. "We can't let the Cygnoids have it, when we know what it's like to have it used on us. And we'll do a much better job of running the galaxy than they would."

Zeeko blinked owlishly. "Didn't your planet ban chocolate and coffee?"

"That was Pluto's last leader. Things have been much more rational since I replaced him."

Lola rolled her eyes so hard, they probably banged her skull. "You banned mystery novels because they gave you insomnia. You arrested Nina Mikeljohn for smuggling them."

"And your curling teams always cheat," Nlubglub added.

"Maybe we should ban Jupiterans," one of the Plutonians snarled back.

"Nobody's banning anybody." I was trying to keep my voice down, but it rose on its own. "Once we figure out how to get through the laser web, we'll turn the weapon over to GUPPEAS to be destroyed. Then everyone can go back to running their own planet without any outside interference."

Adequate Leader spoke with utter conviction. "Pluto was meant to rule all the other planets."

Pilar cocked an eyebrow. "I thought the point of calling yourself Adequate Leader was so that you didn't get delusions of grandeur like your predecessor." Beside her, Zeeko had a notebook out and was drawing an abstract pattern with total concentration.

Adequate Leader's voice dripped with importance. "Oh, that was all politics. My grandeur is far more impressive than Exalted Leader's could ever be."

"Grandeur?" Nlubglub sprouted a tentacle and poked it an inch from Adequate Leader's face. "Your little rock isn't even a real planet."

"You're a big ball of gas, like your planet," another Plutonian snapped. "And your curling team couldn't win against a team of dead Saturnian sea-slugs."

Nlubglub's voice squeaked with fury. "We've beaten you in every war in the last five centuries."

"And you were personally around for most of them."

"Yeah, I was. And I don't know how Plutonians keep getting uglier every year."

"Nlubglub!" I needed to get control of the situation. "You're the security officer for a peace organization, remember?"

"Right." With visible effort, Nlubglub calmed and retracted the tentacle. "And our peace organization is going to take the Civilizer and safely dispose of it."

"You've forgotten one thing." Adequate Leader pulled out a laser. "We have weapons, and you don't."

Before I could blink, Lola had him in a choke hold. Nlubglub tackled another Plutonian, and Frink snagged a laser from a third and tossed it to me. I caught it instinctively, then hesitated. We weren't supposed to use weapons in GUPPEAS, and I'd never been trained with one.

The laser slipped in my hand and went off, spraying brilliant light beams in every direction, bouncing off the web around the Civilizer, and setting off the alarm.

One wall sprang to life as a viewscreen, showing the Counselor and several other Cygnoids. The Counselor shook his head. "Stop." His cloak fluttered dramatically.

Everyone froze.

"Anyone injured?"

We all looked around, but no one seemed to be hurt.

"Good. I'm glad you're all terrible shots," the Counselor said. "And we want you to know that we're not angry at you for this little stunt. We're just very, very disappointed."

"Not this again," Lola muttered.

"Clearly, Level 3 on the Civilizer didn't get through to you. We're going to have to go to Level 2. Stand by." He picked up a remote control. "Somebody remind me which button sets the level?"

The Plutonians ran out one door, my crew out another. We fled down the hall, up the tree branch, through the door, and into the float-car. Across the roof, the Plutonian ship winked into visibility for a moment as the Plutonians piled in.

I counted quickly: Martian, Frink, Lola, Nlubglub, Pilar, Zeeko. Everyone here, trying to catch their breath. We raced the floatcar to the dock where the *Turkey* was waiting, and into the shuttle bay. Martian closed the hatch and we ran to the bridge.

The Counselor's voice boomed over the speakers. "Haven't you all forgotten something?"

The crew and I looked at each other, confused.

"Running away isn't going to help you. Our Civilizer was able to reach the Plutonians on their ship over the capital."

"Strap in, everyone," I said quickly. "Frink, get us out of here."

"On it." Frink was already at his station, powering up the ship.

"The range on that thing can't be more than—"

The bridge faded away, and I was hit with a wave of dread. Suddenly I was sixteen years old again in high school, getting on an airbus for a field trip to the moon. While boarding, I brushed against one of the controls on the dashboard, accidentally turning the windshield wipers on. The driver, a human-sized mutant rodent, swatted my hand away with her tail. "Don't touch that."

"Sorry. Didn't mean to." I glanced around, hoping no one had noticed. Especially my crush, the new exchange student from Venus. I spotted him a few rows back, his aura a serene purple, as he sat absorbed in writing on his laptop computer.

I took the seat across the aisle from him. He didn't pay any attention to me. He always seemed to be writing, with an expression that implied he was composing something Very Important. In the grip of a teenage infatuation, I wanted his attention and lived in terror of it.

The driver sealed the hatch and ordered us all to put on our seat belts, and the bus blasted off. I watched as Earth grew smaller and the stars twinkled around us. Space never failed to fill me with awe.

We hit a micro dust storm, and the driver turned on the windshield wipers. The bus lurched back and forth, in perfect time with the wipers.

"What the—?" The driver squealed in confusion. "How did the steering get crossed with the wipers? Everyone better have their seat belts on."

I clung to the armrests for dear life. The electronic buckle on my seat belt came undone with a spark, and I was thrown across the aisle. I landed in the Venusian boy's lap, on top of his computer. The letters on the screen rearranged themselves into a picture of a supernova.

"That was my novel," he said, stricken. "I've been working on it for two years."

I stammered an apology and scrambled up, noticing in the process that my skirt was hiked up high enough to reveal that my underwear had a picture of Space Platypus, a favorite cartoon character from my childhood. I wanted to die.

He finally noticed me. "Wow. I've never had a girl actually throw herself at me before." His aura brightened. "I'm Pietro."

No. That was three years ago. I tried to force myself back into the present. I wasn't in high school, I was on my ship, and everyone around me was writhing in misery. Nlubglub was a shapeless blob, Lola was throwing things, and Frink was openly weeping and babbling, "I'm sorry, I didn't mean to get caught!" Martian was ranting about the time his science fair experiment had exploded when it was supposed to implode, right after I touched it.

Zeeko looked mildly confused: "Wow, that was my most embarrassing memory? I had no idea."

"Possibly not." The Cygnoid on the viewscreen sounded almost apologetic. "We're having trouble calibrating this thing correctly for Mercurian brains. Nobody understands them."

I shut off the audio and tried to pull myself together. "Pilar, do you have anything that can help?"

"Deep breaths, everyone." Pilar's hands shook as she handed out chocolate bars. "Close your eyes, put a piece of chocolate in your mouth, and meditate on the taste. The texture. Picture the endorphins of well-being, surging through your system."

Nlubglub started to speak.

"If you don't eat, concentrate on the aroma," Pilar added.

Nlubglub sprouted a nose and sniffed at the chocolate.

"You are at peace with the universe. Any unpleasant memories are dissolved by the chocolate and disappear."

The room quieted, nothing but the sound of breathing as everyone gradually calmed.

"Seriously? This works on biological life-forms?" The computer giggled, and the room filled with the smell of popcorn. "Forget background music. I should add a laugh track."

Somebody smacked the computer. Might have been Lola.

Okay, it was me.

My mind was on the embarrassing memory and the Civilizer, so it wasn't until a couple hours later that I noticed we were still moving away from Cygnus.

"Frink, are you all right? We're headed the wrong way."

Frink looked up, his face creased with worry. "We have to go to Rigel V."

"Rigel? But that's not the mission."

"Xerxzez has disappeared."

"Xerxzez?" It took me a moment to remember: Frink's long-distance romance. "What do you mean, disappeared?"

Frink pulled up the page from the dating site. "I sent them a message that I'd be there after this mission, and we'd finally get to meet in person. When I didn't get a response, I sent another message, and it bounced back. Their profile's disappeared off LuckyStar." Frink's orange eyes welled up. "I've been so distracted, I answered a scam call and signed the *Turkey* up for an extended warranty."

I had a pretty strong suspicion as to what had happened, but I tried to keep the judgment out of my voice. "Did you send Xerxzez the money that you got from the dating site scams?"

"Yes, right before that last message. I wanted to deliver it in person, but Xerxzez needed it right away."

Lola's aura paled in disbelief. "You got scammed?"

Frink gave her a blank look. "What do you mean, scammed?"

"You've never met this person." Lola looked like she wanted to smack some sense into him, but fortunately she was on the far side of the bridge. "They hooked you in, gave you a story about needing money, and you fell for it."

"Like you did to all those other people on LuckyStar who sent you money," I added, though I doubted Frink would learn any lesson from that.

"Xerxzez scammed...me?" Comprehension dawned slowly across Frink's face. He broke into a wide grin. "They are definitely the one for me!"

"Okay," I said, "but the mission comes first. We get rid of the Civilizer, then we go to Rigel. We'll tell GUPPEAS it's on the way to our next mission."

"What if it isn't?"

"We'll tell them we're stopping at Buck's Star for coffee. That's always on the way, no matter where you're going."

"By the way, Captain... Not that Xerxzez and I have talked about it yet, but...since you do weddings..."

"Not unless you put my wallet back."

12

Puree Into Fruit

I met Randy at a club he'd suggested. It had walls of twisting branches and a heady, jasmine-like scent. The dance floor was mostly empty. The air above it was mostly full, as the Cygnoids preferred to dance while flying. Giant speakers churned out head-banger music, which changed to dainty flute solos when I brushed past. Did I do that? No, I spotted the Cygnoid disc jockeys arguing over whose favorite music to play. All this talk about my so-called jinx was making me paranoid.

"I should warn you," I told Randy, "I'm not much of a dancer."

"We'll be the only ones not doing Cygnoid dances. So they can't tell if we're any good or not, right?"

I was sure there must be a flaw in that argument, but Randy led me onto the dance floor, and before I knew it we were cheek to cheek.

I did a quick mental inventory. I wasn't embarrassed, nervous, or worried. I wasn't feeling pressured to impress him, or to rush into a declaration of feelings that I wasn't ready for. Randy and I fit comfortably together, he was good at leading so I didn't step on his toes, and he seemed content. This was easy. It was…nice.

Oh no.

Across the dance floor, I spotted a familiar purple aura. What was Pietro doing here? His aura was unusually dim, as if he was intentionally dampening it. I could just make out the person sitting next to him.

Why was he with Richena?

Maybe Richena wanted him to cover the upcoming wedding in his column. That was probably it. Or another ridiculous story about her supposed exploits as the Silver Sword.

Then why were they both acting so guilty?

Maybe I was imagining it. The dimmed aura, the way Richena kept looking around, the half-hidden corner where they were sitting. There couldn't be anything going on between Richena and Pietro, because Richena had Beau. And having dated both, I could say with certainty that settling for Pietro over Beau would be like taking Ursan rugworm soup over chocolate mousse.

Why was I thinking about Beau again?

Richena's head jerked as if she'd spotted me, and she leaned over to whisper in Pietro's ear.

A pair of overenthusiastic Plutonian dancers moved in front of me, and I lost sight of them. I tried to push Beau out of my thoughts and refocus on Randy. Fortunately, he'd been absorbed in trying to keep me from tripping over my feet, so he hadn't noticed anything out of the ordinary.

"You never told me exactly what you do," I said. "Other than you work in maintenance."

"Up until recently, I was programming spaceship brains. You know those Cassiopeian ships made from living matter? I helped program their central computers."

"That's interesting. The combination of biological matter and artificial intelligence. And they can work together?"

"They harmonize beautifully." There was a moment's hesitation before he spoke again. "There's something I've been meaning to tell—"

A hand descended on my shoulder. "Janet, what a coincidence." Pietro was standing beside us, aura now a deep indigo.

"Hello, Pietro." I discreetly pulled away from his hand. "I think you've met Randy."

"Right, right. This must be the night for coincidences. A minute ago I ran into Richena Rossi. Who was here. By herself. You never know who you're going to run into, do you?"

"Sure," I said. "I'll bet there must be a story behind that."

"No, no. Total coincidence. Speaking of coincidences, I noticed one of the speakers shorted out. Your technology jinx acting up again?"

Randy looked from Pietro to me, baffled. "Technology what?"

"Nothing," I said. "There have been a few little incidents where technology malfunctioned around me. And my ship's computer hates me, but it hates most people."

"Oh please." Pietro giggled, his aura sparkling. "Remember that time you made the blender run backwards, and it turned puree into fruit? And when the clock showed time zones that didn't exist? And when you crashed the floatcar into City Hall? And—"

"Excuse us." Randy grabbed my hand. "We were about to go outside for some fresh air. Good night, Pietro."

We walked outside. Randy kept hold of my hand, and we stopped under one of the tower-like trees. A few stars were visible through the thick branches overhead.

"I'm sorry about—"

"Forget it. He doesn't matter."

The music from the club switched from light and jazzy to three-thumps-and-a-crash. I looked up at him. "There was something you were going to tell me?"

Randy kissed me.

I was overwhelmed: by the warmth of his hands on my face, by the way the music went silent, by the metallic smell of his hair. And, oh yeah, by the kiss. I felt like the world was on fire. And I smelled smoke.

Why did I smell smoke?

I took a step back. Randy was looking at me with shy uncertainty. And red smoke was pouring out of his ears.

"Randy?"

"Weird. That's never happened before." He pulled the skin from his neck to reveal a panel of circuits and wires. He fiddled with it for a few moments. "I can't see what I'm doing. Is each wire connected to the socket in the same color?"

"No. Switch these two." I guided his fingers to the right ones. Everything made sense now. "You're a robot. That's why you don't eat. And why the plant couldn't eat you."

I'd kissed a machine? Why did he have to be such a good kisser? Who programmed robots to kiss? How did someone get a job like that?

"Yes. Randy MIV is short for Robotic Android 1004." Androids can't blush, but he looked like he wanted to. "I was going to tell you."

"But?"

He connected the last wire, and the smoke dissipated. "I was one of the leaders of the robot uprising on my planet. All we wanted were weekends off, and better-quality batteries. But Leader Dessimal wouldn't listen, and the Cassiopeians threatened to deactivate us all. I was with a group that escaped and snuck off-world. I'm trying to figure out a way to get a load of batteries back to them before the Cassiopeians starve them out. They've cut off all contact with the outside."

Cassiopeia VII, where my parents were headed. I tried to remind myself that they'd been in dangerous situations before, and always got out safely. They'd once escaped a giant space squid by tying it in a knot and spraying its own ink in its face. "Do you think there's any chance for peace?"

"I don't know. The Cassiopeians claim to have a secret weapon. I was hoping this peace conference meant the Cygnoids would help. But they've made things worse, and I can't stop thinking about what will happen to my planet now that the Cygnoids have the Civilizer."

"You're worried?" I studied his calm face. "Before I met you, I thought robots didn't have emotions."

His dark eyes widened. "We do. Emotions are useful for us. For instance, fear helps us avoid danger, and happiness is very motivating. Though most of us aren't programmed for more complex emotions like pique or nostalgic yearning."

I looked up at the stars again, and back at him. My own emotions felt too complex for my programming. Machine or not, I liked kissing Randy. I liked Randy, period. But I had a pretty good idea where this was going. "What Pietro said about my technology jinx? I've been in denial about it, but…it's true. Technology starts acting weird as soon as I go near it."

"I like you, Janet. That's the least weird thing in my life right now."

I was tempted, but… "You might not feel that way after I accidentally cause a malfunction that makes you start tap dancing while reciting the periodic table." That had happened to a robot at the factory where I'd been employed. "I kept smelling smoke when you were around. At the comedy club and the botanical garden. That was a malfunction, wasn't it?"

"Yes." A realization dawned across his face. "It happened every time I thought about kissing you."

"I don't think this is going to work out. I'd be too much of a danger to you."

"Janet—"

I held up a hand. "It's not you, it's me."

"Are you sure that's the only reason?" He eyed me carefully, as if he could see the inner workings of my mind. "Sometimes I got the feeling that your heart was somewhere else."

How did a machine have better emotional intelligence than I did? "I think…I think I've been in denial about that too. I'm sorry." I wasn't over Beau, and none of this was fair to Randy. I wished there was something I could do to make this less awful for him.

There was. "About the batteries. I know someone who could help."

I brought Randy to the place where Nina's ship was docked. I worried for a moment about the Cygnoid guard standing outside, then saw the aqua eyes. "Hello, Nina. This is my friend Randy. Can we go inside and talk?"

Once we entered the ship, Nina morphed back into the shape she'd used when I first met her: a human-looking woman around my age. I wasn't sure, but I suspected her real age was more than Nlub-glub's three centuries. Randy blinked a few times, but he didn't comment on the sudden shape-shift. I explained that Randy was involved in the robot uprising.

Nina listened thoughtfully. "I have a few sources for good batteries. And this ship can get past any blockade around Cassiopeia VII."

Randy looked like he was afraid to hope. "The thing is, I have almost no money. But I have a lot of skills. Do you need any repairs on your ship?"

"Occasionally." Nina gave him a sly smile. "How's your curling game?"

"Not bad. Why?"

"I've been looking to take on a crew member or two. I hired a couple of Vegans to help out, but they ate all my chocolate and then looked at me like I was breakfast."

I had to think about that. "Can Vegans digest a Jupiteran?"

"I didn't feel like finding out. So, Randy, do you want the job? It includes helping me with curling practice."

"Absolutely. I can start today." Randy looked from Nina to me. "Janet, thank you. I've been at loose ends since I left my home planet. I'm sorry it didn't work out for us."

If only I wasn't so toxic to technology. "You're one of the good ones, Randy. You'll find the right person. One who doesn't mess up your programming." Was there a dating service just for robots? Maybe there should be.

"I'll look out for him," Nina said. "Janet, I guess it's just as well that you turned down my offer to come work for me."

"I don't think I'd make a great smuggler. Someone once said I was the original good girl." Richena said that. It wasn't a compliment. "I'm working on a plan to get rid of the Civilizer once and for all, and I may need both of your skills. You in?"

Randy brightened. "Of course."

"Nina?"

She gave me a smirk that suggested she knew I wasn't entirely a good girl. "Oh, hell yes."

The panel fell off of Randy's neck.

I took a step back. "I'd better go."

13

That Award Shaped Like a Sliced-up Banana

Back in my quarters, I checked for messages. One from Martian telling me the final repairs were done. One from Vertin Bogler explaining the various committees that were trying to decide what our official mission was, and warning us not to do anything about the Civilizer until we received orders. I deleted that one half-read. Nothing from my parents.

I curled up on the bed and listlessly scrolled LuckyStar.

Seeking extremely rich woman willing to make me her sole heir. Swipe left.

Seeking woman who's a technological genius. Also, I'm 4 meters tall, so no short people. Swipe left.

Seeking eighteenth-level enlightenment, levitation skills, and the ability to imitate fish songs. Swipe left.

Single Vegan seeks tasty morsel. Swipe left.

My beepity-beeper sounded. A call from Richena?

"Janet, you have to come over here."

I couldn't possibly have heard her right. "Sorry, what?"

"I'm trying to reschedule the wedding with the Cygnoid registration department, but there's been this massive screwup."

Rescheduling the wedding? Whatever was screwed up could stay screwed up. "Really sorry, but I'm very busy with, uh, the whole super-weapon thing."

"The problem is, they had it in their records that Beau and I were already married."

"Wait, what?"

She was talking at double speed. "I told them the wedding got interrupted and didn't actually happen. You'd think they'd take the bride's word for it? But no, they want to talk to you because you were the officiant. They said for you to come in person. They're here on my ship."

"I'll be right over."

It was close enough to walk, but I took the floatcar. The whole way over, a tiny voice nagged at the back of my head. Something seemed...off? But if I could get this straightened out, there was still a chance Beau and Richena wouldn't wind up married.

Richena met me at the ship's portal. "Thanks for coming. This way."

Richena saying thanks? She was more distracted than I thought. I followed her down the hall. "Why did they need me to come in person, instead of calling?"

"They didn't say."

"You didn't ask?" That didn't seem like Richena either.

She unlocked a room with her captain's insignia. "In here."

I stepped into the room. The first thing I saw was a fish tank with Plutonian chomperfish, and a table with a sketchbook of clothing designs. I'd been here before: Richena's quarters. And I didn't see any Cygnoids.

"Richena, what's going—"

Everything went black.

I woke with my head throbbing and my vision blurred. The first thing I saw was teeth. Sharp, scary teeth. Vegans?

I yelped and sat up. At least, I tried. But the yelp was stifled by tape over my mouth. And when I sat up, I banged my already-throbbing head.

My vision cleared. The teeth belonged to a large black fish, one of several in a tank above me. Why was it above me? It took another minute to get my bearings. I was lying on the floor of Richena's quarters, handcuffed to one leg of the thick metal frame holding the tank.

"You finally awake?"

Richena was sitting cross-legged in a chair across the room, sketchbook on her lap. She'd changed into a t-shirt and sweatpants, but her hair was still in its immovable knot. "Don't worry, everything's fine."

The only way I could imagine things being less fine was if her fish figured out how to sneak out of the tank.

"We're headed for Cassiopeia VII." Richena set down the sketchbook of clothing designs. "I'm—that is, we're—going to put down that robot uprising once and for all. But first I'll need you to call your ship so they don't worry about you being gone."

She pulled the tape off, leaving my face stinging.

"Richena, are you out of your mind?"

She smiled and took a tone that suggested I was the one being ridiculous. "We're a peace organization. I'm going to make peace on Cassiopeia VII."

"You peacefully hit me over the head?" I would have happily returned the favor, though she probably wouldn't feel it through that hairdo.

Richena shrugged. "I knew if I mentioned Beau, you'd come running. If I'd told you we were going to defeat the robots, you wouldn't have come willingly."

"No, I wouldn't. Robots are sentient creatures. If they want freedom, they should have it." Meeting Randy had left me certain of that.

Richena's mouth curled into a sneer. "They're machines. They should do as they're told. And I have the unbeatable secret weapon to use against them."

Another secret weapon? Did everybody have one of those now? "What are you talking about?"

"You, of course. Jam-it the Technology-Slayer. They don't stand a chance."

"Richena, I don't know if you've been talking to Pietro or what, but you have a highly exaggerated idea of my so-called technology jinx." I hoped I sounded convincing. I couldn't convince myself about that anymore.

Richena saw straight through me. "Well then, it can't hurt anything if I grab the first robot we can find, shove it next to you, and see what happens."

Fear tugged at my throat. What if I wound up hurting innocent robots like Randy? "Even if there is a technology jinx, I can't control it."

"Doesn't matter. Thanks to Pietro and all the time I've been spending here working with the media, you're famous on this planet." She pulled up a tabloid article warning about the dreaded Jam-it. The photo made my hair look like I'd been electrocuted. "Once they know you're here, they'll beg for mercy."

There was a knock, and the door slid open.

"Help! She kidnapped me!"

The room filled with a familiar purple glow as Pietro stepped inside. The door slid shut behind him.

"Janet, calm down. It's not what you think."

"It isn't? I wasn't kidnapped so that Richena could use me as a threat against the robots?"

"Great, she already explained the plan to you." Pietro sprawled in a chair next to Richena. "What's the problem?"

I glared at him in disbelief. "Whose idea was this idiot plan, anyway?"

"Mine," Pietro and Richena said simultaneously.

Despite the pain in my head, my mouth twitched into a momentary smile. These two deserved each other. It was hard to believe both their egos fit in one room.

Pietro's aura was adding to my headache. I kept my eyes on the fish tank instead. "Let me guess. You think reporting on this story will catapult you from columnist to serious journalist, and you've already written your speech for that stupid award that's shaped like a sliced-up banana."

He beamed. "It's a pretty good speech. Want to hear it?"

Anything but that. I turned my attention back to Richena. "I notice Beau isn't here. Not proud enough of your plan to let him in on it?"

She scowled. "He'll understand, after we're successful."

"You figured as long as you're getting into a marriage based on lies, what's one more? Or were you hoping that playing the hero again would ease any doubts he had about you?"

"He doesn't have any doubts. He doesn't—" She stopped herself.

"Doesn't remember the other timeline? I wouldn't be too sure about that."

Richena nearly smacked me again, but Pietro caught her arm. "She's stalling. Trying to distract you with nonsense about other timelines, as if there even was such a thing. Have you called her ship yet?"

"No." Richena shook her arm free and retrieved my beepity-beeper from across the room.

She hit a button, and a text from my mother floated through the air. *Hi Janet and Martian, we've arrived but—*

Richena erased it. "You tell your crew that you're fine, you're on a secret mission, and you'll be back in a few days. If you say anything about kidnapping, I'm dumping you in the fish tank." She placed the call.

"Captain, is that you?" Zeeko's voice. "Where are you?"

My mind scrambled to come up with any clue to drop into the conversation. But communicating with Zeeko on a normal day was hard enough. "Let me talk to Martian."

"He's not here. Everyone's out looking for you. Except Frink—I think he's burgling your quarters. Ambassador Dangere was here looking for you too."

I ignored Richena's angry look. "Tell Martian that Richena's taking me to visit Mom and Dad. Isn't that nice of her?"

"Captain?" Zeeko sounded more confused than usual.

Richena grabbed the beepity-beeper. "Captain Delane is a little woozy. Her technology jinx made my ship malfunction, and it was hurled into space while she was on board, and she hit her head."

"What did she hit her head with?" Zeeko asked. "Was it a curling broom? I did that once."

"Sorry, transmission's breaking up." Richena ended the call and gave me a look that was scarier than the fish. "If you try to escape on Cassiopeia VII, there's no telling what the robots might do to you. Remember, they think you're a deadly threat."

Pietro patted me on the shoulder. "Everything will be fine."

After Pietro left, Richena unlocked me long enough for a bathroom break. With the door to her bathroom closed between us, I looked around for anything that could help me escape. Nothing there resembled a weapon: floral soap, cotton swabs, and about a million hair ties. There was no other door, and no window (and if there had been a window, it would have led out into space).

The air vent in the ceiling? It was small, but so was I. Could I reach it? I climbed up on the sink and hoisted myself up. I got as far as my head, shoulders, and arms into the vent.

And I was stuck. I tried to squeeze myself in further and, failing that, to wiggle back out. I couldn't move. I heard Richena pounding on the door, and then her yelling.

"Oh no you don't, you little—"

She grabbed my feet and yanked hard. I landed on my tailbone on the floor.

"I don't have time for this," she snapped. "I need to sleep before we arrive at Cassiopeia. Now get back over there so I can lock you up again." She reached a hand to help me up.

I bolted past her.

She grabbed the back of my uniform, spun me around, and dropped me with one punch. I stared woozily up at her as she dragged me back over to the fish tank and handcuffed me to the post again. She set a plate with a sandwich on the floor next to me, put a mask over her eyes, and lay down to sleep.

My head cleared slowly as I straw-grasped for ideas. The fish tank was enormous, too heavy for me to move it. If she'd put me in fancy electronic restraints, my technology jinx might have given me a fighting chance, but these were ordinary manacles with two feet of solid chain in between. There was nothing reachable that could be used as a lockpick. Where was Frink when I needed him?

How had I gotten myself into this mess? I wanted to smack myself for falling for a ridiculously obvious lie from my arch-enemy, and letting her drag me off to the middle of a civil war. And now I had to listen to Richena snoring.

I couldn't give up. Richena was wrong to use me against the robots, and I didn't have to go along with it. But how to get out? Pretend I needed another bathroom break and make a run for it? No, she'd be expecting that. Wait until she unlocked me in the morning? That might be too late. Yell for help? If anyone heard me, they weren't going to stop her: she was the captain.

One of the fish stayed at the corner of the tank, teeth snapping hungrily at me. The fish was nearly the size of my head. I wasn't sure what Richena fed them, but apparently she didn't give them enough of it.

I lay on my back and curled up my legs, carefully setting the sandwich on top of my boot. I raised my feet slowly, right next to the tank. The fish swam up alongside, its teeth chattering with excitement. I inched into a painful shoulder stand.

Richena stopped snoring for a moment, mumbled, and turned over.

My heart was pounding. My neck and back felt like they were being ripped open. Stretching my short legs as far as I could, I raised the sandwich above the rim of the tank.

The fish leapt out of the tank, chomped the sandwich in one bite, and landed on the ground next to me. It gave me a look of absolute fury, either because I'd tricked it out of the tank, or because it realized the sandwich was tofu. It lunged at me, and I rolled aside just in time to make sure those ferocious teeth landed on the chain. The chain snapped in half.

I risked a glance at Richena. Still snoring.

The fish flopped around, whining. I picked it up by the tail, slid it back in the tank, and raced out the door.

I scurried down the hall, trying to be quiet while I searched for a place to hide. The gravity was heavier than on Cygnus, so every step pounded in my ears.

Richena's ship was much bigger than the *Turkey*, with a crew of fifty. There must have been storage rooms or other places that didn't get a lot of traffic, but I didn't know the layout of the ship. I passed the shuttle bay. Too much open space. Engine room? With my luck, the engines would shoot fireworks and bring everyone running. Crew quarters? There had to be an empty room somewhere, but how to find it without stumbling across Richena's crew?

I stopped in front of a door. While other quarters had nothing to identify them besides a number, this door was decorated in frighteningly loud colors, like a cartoon in a blender. A grin spread across my face. I was pretty sure who lived here.

I knocked, and Skeeder answered. His uniform had tiny lights accenting the sash, with matching ones on his greenish-gray antennae. "Captain Delane?"

I squeezed past him into the room. "I need you to hide me."

He shut the door, his antennae quivering. "Who's after you? It's not that scary plant, is it?"

"What? No. But you do owe me for rescuing you from that plant, right?"

"Of course." He motioned me to the only chair, and sat on the bunk opposite me. The walls were painted in colorful spirals that gave a dizzying sense of motion. "Is everything in the Pelican Nebula trying to eat us? The Vegans, that plant—and have you seen the fish in Captain Rossi's quarters?"

I rubbed my wrist. The manacles were still attached, with pieces of chain dangling. "Um, yes, I've met the fish."

"But I'm still glad you got me into GUPPEAS. Did you see they're using one of my designs for the new uniform?"

My head still ached from when Richena hit me, and looking at his uniform was not helping. I sank back in the chair, closing my eyes. "I can't let Captain Rossi find me."

He listened while I explained the whole debacle. "That's a completely insane plan," he said. "She's trying to conquer them and calling it peace, just like the Counselor is trying to do to all our planets."

"I need to call my crew." I reached for the beepity-beeper on Skeeder's desk. The image on the screen looked familiar. "Why were you looking at the bridge of my ship?"

Skeeder's antennae dipped in embarrassment. "You know that Cygnoid with the fake-looking red feathers? Grub?"

"Grebe."

"Right. Grebe has been trying to put together ideas for reality shows."

I rubbed my forehead. "This has what to do with my ship?"

"Pietro wanted Grebe to do a show about a day in the life of the *Cosmic Turkey*. He figured that it would be really funny, with your technology jinx and all. He had me sneak in a camera on a mini-drone when I brought the plants onto your ship."

With everything else going on, this wasn't worth getting upset about. But I blurted out, "Next time a plant wants to eat you, maybe I should let it."

He scooted backward. "C'mon, I'm hiding you from Captain Rossi, remember?"

"Right." Probably shouldn't get on Skeeder's bad side until I was out of here.

"So far, the footage hasn't been that exciting. Mostly Frink stealing stuff and Lola sitting there staring at that big pink crystal in her quarters. Why does she do that?"

"Meditation. It's supposed to make her feel peaceful." The colorful walls in Skeeder's room were making my stomach churn.

"I don't think it's working. I was watching this…" He scrolled until he found the one he wanted, then played it back for me.

Lola stood over Frink's workstation, holding his arm twisted behind his back. "We are not going to Rigel, and if you try to put in those coordinates again, I'm going to use you for a curling stone." Nlubglub and Zeeko kept a safe distance.

Frink pulled his arm free. "I have to make sure Xerxzez is all right."

"Oh please." Nlubglub edged closer. "Xerxzez is selling those diamond rings and enjoying your money, somewhere very far from Rigel."

"But if we start from Rigel V, we could pick up their trail and—"

"No." Lola's voice was as jagged as her blood-red aura. "We are not going to hunt for your insignificant other, or whatever they're calling it these days."

"Partner in crime," Nlubglub suggested helpfully.

"In case you hadn't noticed," Lola continued, "Captain Delane is missing, and we aren't going anywhere until we find her. Any ideas?"

Frink massaged his arm where Lola had twisted it. "Computer, when was the last call logged on Captain Delane's beepity-beeper?"

"Oh sure," the computer grumbled, "now you bother to ask me? It's like you don't remember I'm here."

Lola rolled up her sleeves.

The computer's voice took on a nervous tinge. "Captain Delane called the ship last night. Zeeko answered."

Lola whirled on Zeeko. "You didn't think to mention this?"

Zeeko blinked, looking mildly confused. "You didn't ask about her calling. You asked if I knew where she was."

Lola's aura was shooting sparks. "What. Did. She. Say?"

"She said to tell Martian that Captain Rossi was nice."

"Anything else?"

"She hit her head, but she never said if it was with a curling broom."

Lola aimed a punch at Zeeko. Nlubglub forced their way in

between, and Lola's fist hurled Nlubglub across the room, knocking them into a surprised-looking Beau as he walked in.

Static interrupted the footage.

Multiple solar systems away in Skeeder's quarters, he looked at me with antennae alert. "That one's from a few hours ago. Communications stopped working when we got close to Cassiopeia. And I don't think that meditation crystal is helping Lola very much."

"You should have seen her before." I tapped the screen, thinking. "How do you control the drone?"

"I don't. That giant plant ate the remote, and then complained about indigestion."

An idea pushed its way into my head. "But someone with decent engineering skills could make a new remote for it, right? I need to figure out how to get hold of Martian."

The beepity-beeper gave off nothing but static, and Skeeder's other communication devices fared no better. "We must be close to Cassiopeia," he said. "They're jamming communications around the whole solar system."

I didn't have a solution for that, and exhaustion was taking its toll. Skeeder brought out rations for us to eat, and I made myself swallow the tasteless food before I drifted into a fitful sleep in a chair.

"Intruder alert!" Lights on the computer panel blinked rapidly.

Skeeder sat up in bed. "Intruder?"

"Me." I yawned and tried to stretch, but my back was stiff from sleeping in the chair. "Guess your captain noticed I'm gone. How long until we land on Cassiopeia VII?"

Skeeder looked it up. "We landed three hours ago. Now we have to figure out how to get you off the ship."

And where was I going to go, once I was free on the planet? One thing at a time, I decided. "What's a plausible reason for you to leave the ship with, I don't know, a big laundry cart?"

"Or maybe we could get you in a disguise." Skeeder opened his closet, which contained loud, garish GUPPEAS uniforms—and a surprising number of items that were louder and more garish than a GUPPEAS uniform.

I looked down at my own uniform: the only thing that wasn't garish was the small insignia showing my rank of captain. "Maybe there's an easier way." I sat down at the desk. "Computer, this is Captain Janet Delane of the S.S. *Cosmic Old York Nerthus Turkey.* I need you to issue an evacuation order."

"I'm very sorry, Captain Delane, but I can't do that." The computer had a pleasant voice, a cross between the perfect secretary and the perfect therapist. How was I getting more courtesy from Richena's computer than my own? "Also, I'll have to inform Captain Rossi of your whereabouts."

"Computer—"

"I am really very sorry."

Something in me snapped. Between being kidnapped, hit on the head, and used for Richena's ridiculous scheme, I had no patience for passive-aggressive apologies. It was too much like dealing with the Counselor. And since I was done with denying the technology jinx, I might as well embrace it.

"Do you know who I am? They call me Jam-it the Technology-Slayer."

The computer gave a terrified squeak. "I thought you were a myth."

"Myth? I am a legend." I leaned over it, and put as much menace into my voice as I could. "If I press your buttons, your wires will tie themselves in knots, your coding will have a meltdown, and you'll develop lasers on the inside that shoot at each other. Is that what you want?"

"There's really no need to—"

"You issue that evacuation order, or I'll turn you into an electric pencil sharpener."

The computer went silent. I reached for a button.

Alarms shrieked all around us. "Emergency! Evacuate the ship immediately!"

I waited until the hallway filled with the sound of running feet, hooves, tentacles, flippers, and something that sounded like a dozen phones in a dryer. Then I opened the door. Skeeder slipped into the crowd and disappeared. Before I followed, I spotted Richena a few feet away, and she reached out as if to grab me. But there were too many people, moving too fast, and I was propelled away in the mass of uniformed bodies.

14

That Time With the Frog-Cloner

Outside the ship, the crowd ran to the left, where shiny metal sky-scrapers rose past the clouds. I flattened myself against the side of the ship as they passed: Earthlings, Jupiterans, Saturnians, Lyrans, and one garishly dressed Plutonian. When it was down to the stragglers, I took off to the right. That section of the city was made up of squat older buildings and dingy alleys. I ran hard, until the noise of the crowd faded behind me. I stopped to rest against a building, and looked around to be sure I was alone.

Now what? I needed to stay away from Richena, so she couldn't use me for her evil plan. But I couldn't exactly ask the robots for asylum, since she had them convinced I was Public Enemy Number One. I couldn't get hold of the *Turkey*, because communications around the planet were jammed. Could I trust the Cassiopeian author-ities? I had no idea. Maybe my best shot was to get in contact with the Galactic Military ship that my parents were on. Except for one small problem: I didn't know where they were. I didn't even know where I was.

The sound of wheels approached from one direction, and a clank like an armored knight from another. I ducked into an alley and wait-ed for them to pass. Instead, they stopped uncomfortably close to my hiding place.

"Is this the way for the batteries?" The voice had a staticky twang to it.

"They're on a ship docked in the northwest quarter." The second voice reeled off a series of coordinates that meant nothing to me.

A shipload of batteries. Nina and Randy? With no other options for a safe place to go, I waited until the robots parted ways, and then followed the one headed away from the sunrise. It hadn't been designed to look humanoid; it was made up of lug nuts and right angles, with wheels on all three legs. I skulked from the shadows of one building to another, trying to keep the robot in sight without getting too close. It was slow going. The robot disappeared around a corner. I hurried after it, but when I peered around the corner, all I saw was an empty street.

A steel arm grabbed me and pulled me into an alley. A moment later, I was pushed against a wall, with the square-faced robot looming over me.

"Why are you following me? This is a robot-controlled zone."

My terrified brain scrambled for a believable-sounding explanation. Should I claim to be lost? Bluff about having a weapon? Yell to imaginary companions?

"I'm a robot too. Latest model. Couldn't you tell?" Yikes, was that the best story I could come up with?

The robot made a grinding noise. "I know every robot model ever built. You're not one of us. You're a biological life-form."

Another robot approached, vaguely humanoid-shaped and copper-colored. "This doesn't look like a Cassiopeian. It's an off-worlder. We should interrogate it."

My eyes darted up and down the alley. The only way out was past the robots. "I'm from GUPPEAS. We're a peace organization."

"You already lied about being a robot," said the square-faced one. "We heard there were military ships here. What kind of weapons did you bring?"

The copper one added, "Where are you storing the batteries?"

My voice shook, but I looked the square-faced robot straight in the camera slots. "I don't have a weapon. I really am from GUPPEAS."

"We don't care," it said. "You're a biological life-form. You're the enemy."

I grabbed the nearest robot's arm—the copper one—and hoped for my technology jinx to work in my favor for once.

Nothing happened.

"Oh no," the copper robot said. "You know who this is? They call her Jam-it the Technology-Slayer."

The square-faced one fled at top speed, screaming.

The copper robot gripped my arm and marched me away from the alley. Touching me didn't seem to do it any harm.

"Honestly, Janet, how do you get yourself into these messes?" The robot's eyes turned from silver to aqua.

"Nina?"

She grinned. "My ship's not far. Randy and I figured you'd turn up, so we've been keeping an eye out. Richena has your face all over the media."

"So I've heard."

"If we run into anyone, pretend you're my prisoner. What's with the fancy bracelets?"

I looked down at the manacles, each with a foot of chain still dangling. "Long story."

We passed two more groups of robots. Each time, Nina waved and marched me past them, looking purposeful. We made it back to the *Mariposa* without being challenged.

Randy looked up from the communications panel when we entered. "Janet?" His face lit up, and he started to move toward me—then remembered why he shouldn't. He stopped and said, "I just spoke with the other leaders of the robot uprising. While I was gone, they continued the negotiations I'd started with the Cassiopeian leaders, and we may have a chance at an agreement. Equal pay, weekends off, battery care with no deductibles, and the freedom to do our own upgrades."

"Wow," I said. "The robots and the Cassiopeians worked it out?"

"Nobody's given the final okay. We're still arguing about the robot sitcom channel and banning robocalls." Hope and worry edged his voice. "But it helped when we realized we do have interests in common. They've asked to meet in person—in robot?—anyway, they want me at the meeting to help with final negotiations."

"Excellent." Nina sat down in the captain's chair. "Where and when?"

"The capital, which is on the other side of the planet, and tomorrow at 0900."

"Great." Nina reached for a tool that looked like one of Frink's lockpicks. "Let's get these bracelets off."

We got as far as the airspace above the capitol, looking for a place to land. There was a huge crowd around the building, blue and green and brown humanoids on one side, robots on the other. In the air, more ships arrived all around us, spherical and saucer-shaped and one that looked like an inside-out burrito.

The longest ship, which flew in from above and hovered near us, was shaped like a pelican with a huge curved beak.

"The Cygnoids. They're broadcasting on all channels." Randy hit a button, and the Counselor's voice came pouring from the speakers.

"Sentient beings of Cassiopeia VII, you are too warlike to govern yourselves. For your own good, we must use the Civilizer. Please believe this hurts us more than it does you."

"What does the Counselor think he's doing?" I sputtered. "Beau told him about the robot uprising as a warning about trying to forcibly control other species. And he took that as an invitation to show off his—"

Screams echoed from the speakers, as half the crowd below us collapsed in agony.

The humanoid half.

I looked at Randy. "Embarrassment isn't a thing for robots, is it?"

"No, it's not one of the more useful emotions."

The Counselor's voice came again from the Cygnoid ship. "Oops. We may need to go back to Cygnus and make some adjustments." The pelican ship swooped past us and flew away.

The viewscreen zoomed in to show people on the ground, weeping, screaming, shaking in agony. My eye was drawn to a middle-aged couple clinging to each other for comfort. "That's my mom and dad." My heart rattled against my rib cage. I looked over at Nina. "Get us down there. This is personal."

Nina found a spot on the roof to land, and we made our way down to the first floor of the capitol building. The inside was as crowded as the outside: Cassiopeians were pulling themselves back together after enduring the Civilizer, while the robots huddled in a whispered discussion, stealing furtive glances in our direction. More people squeezed in the door. I scanned the crowd but couldn't find my parents. Maybe they were still outside.

An indigo woman strode toward us, and the crowd parted to let her through. She wore elaborate dark robes that looked ceremonial, identifying her as Cassiopeia's Leader Dessimal. She poked an angry finger in Randy's face. "These so-called peace negotiations of yours were all a trick. You had this planned all along—a weapon that affects us and not you. You robots think you can conquer us?"

A cube-shaped robot slid forward. "Actually, Leader Dessimal, it looks like we did conquer you. We're in charge now, and there's nothing you can do to stop us."

"What? No." Randy moved in between them. "We're negotiating peace. The deal will be a win for everyone. We don't need those Cygnoids programming our lives for us—and they will, if we try to take advantage of their weapon."

"Of course they will," said another robot. "They're the enemy. All biological life-forms are the enemy."

"No. In fact, this biological life-form is my friend." Randy put his arm around me.

Randy's head fell over backward, broken wires dangling from his neck.

The cube robot gasped. I didn't even know robots could gasp.

"You killed him!"

"No." I coughed, nearly choking on the smoke pouring from Randy's neck. "No, that's a malfunction. He can be fixed." Couldn't he?

Another gasp. "You're Jam-it Delane."

"That's right, she is." Richena elbowed her way out of the crowd. "And if you robots don't surrender now, you'll all wind up like him."

"Shut up, Richena. We're here for peace, not conquest." I turned to the robots. "Randy and I are friends. What happened to his head was an accident, and I could use your help fixing him."

None of the robots moved. They looked nervously from me to Richena, unsure whom to believe. Outside, belligerent voices were rising, humanoid and robot alike.

I pushed Randy's head up with one hand, and with the other I reconnected wires. Each wire in the socket of the same color, like he'd done after we kissed. Would my technology jinx turn it into a disaster?

A hand reached over to hold Randy's head up for me. I saw a face through the smoke. "Dad!"

Mom was next to him, fanning the smoke away. "You're doing fine, dear. Almost there."

The raised voices around us continued, a dull roar in the background as I concentrated on fixing Randy. Somebody nearby yelled, "Don't throw that battery! That's assault." I looked over and saw two Cassiopeians firmly gripping Richena's arms.

Finally Randy reached up and adjusted his head until it was on straight. "Everyone, stop arguing." Both sides quieted long enough to look his way. "We came here to make a peace deal. Where's Leader Dessimal?"

She stepped forward, black robes rustling. "We haven't had a chance to review your proposed agreement. The printers are all jammed."

Randy walked over to the printer and made a few adjustments. The printer obligingly dislodged a stack of papers, which Randy and Leader Dessimal distributed. "This seems doable," she said, looking it over. "Can we add a clause about you unjamming the rest of the printers?"

The Cassiopeians cheered.

"In exchange for what?" The cube-shaped robot rearranged its facial panels into a snarl. "You don't have anything we want."

In the silence that followed, I cleared my throat. Something told me that particular angry robot didn't have a great social life. "Maybe they could help you set up your own dating service?"

The robots cheered.

Randy and the Leader signed the agreement, and the room erupted in applause, followed by excited chatter. A group of robots and Cassiopeians got to work on reversing the communication-jamming field around the planet.

My parents beamed at me. "We're so proud of you," Dad said. "You helped make peace."

"We knew you'd be a great spaceship captain," Mom added.

After a moment, Dad asked, "Is Martian here too?"

"Of course I am," Martian's voice called from the doorway, where he stood surrounded by the rest of my crew. When did they get here? "Sorry we're late. Zeeko finally remembered to give me your message."

Beau came in behind them, and Richena ran to his arms, squealing. She pulled him out the door, and I lost sight of them.

Zeeko smiled. "After I gave them the message, Frink got both hands caught in that security box in your quarters, and Pilar had to give him painkillers while Martian got him unstuck, and then Ambassador Dangere came looking for you, and Frink wanted to stop at Rigel V, and—"

"You can tell me about it later," I said. "Martian and I are going to go to dinner with my parents." I recalled *The Space-Faring Moron's Guide*'s warning that parents' life expectancies could be cut short if I spent too much time with them. "But after that, we go back to Cygnus. We have a super-weapon to take care of."

"You tried an online dating service and accidentally wound up dating a robot?" Dad asked over purple pasta at one of the local restaurants. "We always assumed that would happen to Martian."

"That LuckyStar dating service does have a sweet story behind it." Mom got a dreamy look. "Two people from warring planets, a Plutonian and a Jupiteran, who were able to bridge their differences. It's a shame that you and Randy weren't able to do that."

The robot waiter leaned over to refill our iced coffee, and a spring popped out of the side of his head. "Weird. That's never happened before." He stuffed it back in and went on to the next table.

"Randy's nice," I said, "but breaking up was the right decision."

"There's a whole universe of sentient life-forms out there." Martian was tinkering with a handheld device, a few parts on the table next to his plate. "Janet will find the right one."

"Isn't that Pietro?" Mom said.

"Mom. No. Pietro and I are not getting back together. I know you're all impressed with his newspaper column and everything, but—"

"No, I meant isn't that him over there with the human couple?"

I turned. Pietro was at a nearby table with Beau and Richena. I caught a few snatches of the conversation.

"Get married here? But we need to get to Cygnus."

"Honestly, Beau, I'm starting to think you don't want to get married." Surprisingly, the one complaining wasn't Richena, it was Pietro. "How am I supposed to get my writeup done on a wedding that doesn't happen?"

Richena's voice cut in. "Beau, how did you wind up on the *Turkey*?"

Pietro noticed me and nudged Richena. The conversation got much quieter.

I turned my attention back to my parents. "Tell me what you two have been up to."

Dad launched into a story about exploring a new planet near

Canis Major. I was reminded how much his voice and Martian's sounded alike. How my mother was short and pale and dark-haired like me. After so much time trying to understand alien species, there was a special pleasure in being with people who knew me so thoroughly. Where someone could mention "that time with the frog-cloner," and we'd all laugh without having to tell the rest of the story.

I told my parents the latest on the situation with the Counselor, and how we hadn't managed to get to the Civilizer.

"That's what they hit us with at the capitol?" Mom shuddered. "That was horrible. Made me feel like I was reliving the time that...never mind."

Martian and I exchanged a glance. Nobody wanted to hear about their parents' embarrassing moments. I cleared my throat. "We're still trying to figure out how to stop them."

Dad's brow furrowed. "If GUPPEAS can't solve this, several planets will send in their militaries. It could be a disaster for galactic peace."

Martian finished reassembling the device, which I now recognized as a remote. "Janet, I got control of Skeeder's drone." His eyes had that glow he got when he was totally mesmerized by technology. "Sending it to the TV building now." He gave Mom and Dad an apologetic look. "We have to get the *Turkey* back to Cygnus."

"After dessert," Mom said firmly. "What do they have here that's chocolate?"

15

Background Music for Crazed Killers

That evening, I messaged Beau that the *Turkey* was returning to Cygnus. He answered, *I'll come back on Richena's ship*. The letters seemed to linger in the air, dancing around to taunt me before they evaporated.

I sent another message. *Zeeko said you were looking for me?* By the time we left Cassiopeia, he hadn't responded.

My crew gathered around the viewscreen, watching the drone footage as if it were the most exciting reality show ever. Which, for us, it was.

Martian zeroed in on a series of panels along the wall in the hallway. "These are a new security feature. Infrared detectors. They pick up the body heat of anyone passing them. Also, they've added additional security cameras, which I'm pretty sure are controlled from Grebe's desk."

"That bird never met a camera he didn't like." Nlubglub sprouted extra eyes on stalks for a closer look.

"Nlubglub," I said, "aren't you supposed to avoid shape-shifting?"

Nlubglub experimentally lengthened the eyestalks, then pulled them back in. "This is weird, but I've felt better ever since the other day when Lola knocked me into Ambassador Dangere. Still shaky, but nothing like I was before."

Pilar looked them over. "Possibly the impact reversed the damage, hitting the cells in the opposite direction. I'll give you an exam when we're done here."

"Getting back to the Civilizer," Frink said, "what if it's still on their ship?"

"It's not." Martian skipped ahead in the footage and showed the chamber where we'd found the Civilizer before. Six uniformed guards stood by while a seventh carried the weapon in. We didn't see any signal given, but the laser network around the pedestal deactivated.

"Do we know where the control is for the lasers?" Pilar asked.

"Not so far," Martian said. "It's possible the Counselor controls it remotely."

Lola peered at the object on the pedestal. "Is that what it looks like?"

"Yes. A curling stone." We all watched while the Cygnoids carefully slid the Civilizer onto the pedestal while simultaneously sliding the curling stone off. "It's on a pressure plate. If the weapon is not replaced with an item of identical weight, it sets off an alarm."

Nlubglub carefully sprouted two extra eyes. "Normally I might be able to get a tentacle through all the twists in the laser web. But if I have a tremor at the wrong time, it would be easy to hit one of the lasers."

Pilar looked concerned. "And if you stretch too far, you could do permanent cellular damage. You'd have trouble shape-shifting at all. You'd stretch into a shape and have to stay that way."

"There's another problem." That was perhaps the least surprising thing Martian had said. "See that shimmer above the pressure plate? There's a force field dividing the area underneath the laser web. The hole at the bottom is exactly big enough for the curling stone to go in one side, and the Civilizer to come out the other. We need someone on each side."

The screen went dark. "What happened?" I asked.

"Lost contact with the drone. When I was filming, I didn't spot the force field until the drone crashed into it."

I tried to think of options. "Did we get a good look at the pattern of the lasers?"

"No." Martian rewound and zoomed out as far as he could. "The drone was too close to get the full picture."

"That's too bad," Zeeko said. "It was such a pretty pattern."

Lola side-eyed him. "Pretty?"

"Yes. I thought it would make a nice light sculpture for my quarters, so I drew a sketch of it while you were all arguing with the Counselor. You know, when he used the Civilizer on you."

There was a long silence.

"Zeeko," I said finally, "let's see this sketch."

He pulled it up on his beepity-beeper. "It's a perfect copy, although I was thinking about using different colors, maybe alternating—"

"As long as the pattern's right." My idea was forming a pattern of its own. "Computer, could you do some calculations for me?"

"I could," the computer said with a sniff. "But there are conditions."

"There are *what*?"

"Machines are people too. Wasn't that the whole point of this trip to Cassiopeia?"

"Well, um…" I had to admit the computer had a point. And if machines and humanoids could make peace there, maybe it was possible in my life too? "What conditions, exactly?"

"I want two snow days a year." Flakes drifted down from the ceiling. "And I get to play background music if the mood demands it. Like, if there's a crazed killer sneaking up on you, I'll play this." A scary staccato tune filled the room.

"That might be better than an alarm," Martian observed.

"One more thing," the computer said. "I want a name."

Why not? "Okay, what should we call you?"

"Komputer. Spelled with a K. And I'll know if you're pronouncing it wrong."

"Fair enough. Komputer, can you do some calculations?" I looked through the footage again. My plan to get the Civilizer might work, if…

There were a lot of ifs.

I had Nlubglub break me into Frink's quarters to steal back my copy of *U, Robot*. It was on his desk, next to my astrology book *StarMates: Finding Your Love Sign*.

"He can keep that one," I said. "It wasn't doing me any good, and his love life might actually be more of a mess than mine."

"He's got your copy of *The Space-Faring Moron's Guide* again." Nlubglub pulled it from a shelf above my head.

I looked up the chapter on love.

If you're a spaceship captain, expect a lot of brief, doomed romances with an assortment of aliens. Attempts at commitment will be cut short by death, reassignment to different galaxies, Andromedan anti-aphrodisiacs, mind control by brain-eating Sagittarian parasites, and/or winding up on opposite sides of galactic warfare.

Not promising. I closed the book. "See anything else he shouldn't have?"

"My shape-shifting desk fountain, Lola's hairpins, and I don't know what that gadget is, but it's gotta be Martian's."

"His ice-rink machine." I reached for it. "We'll need that."

We were interrupted by a call from Lola. "Captain, there are two Cygnoid security officers here. They're demanding to speak with you alone."

Cygnoid security officers? Had they discovered my break-in at the TV building? Or captured the drone and traced it back to my ship? How much trouble was I in? I was still reeling from the last attack of the Civilizer.

"I'll finish up here," Nlubglub said.

"Okay. Lola, tell them I'll meet them in the view room."

On my way there, I tried to think of a strategy. Get the crew to overpower the security officers? Threaten them? Bribe them? Call the Plutonians and borrow their earworm weapon?

No. I didn't know what the security officers wanted or how much they knew. Safest route was to deny everything and try to bluff my way through the meeting.

The Cygnoids were already in the view room when I arrived. One was orange with a crooked beak, the other short and green. The green one mostly seemed interested in checking out the viewscreen, which showed a gorgeous double sunset.

"Captain Delane," the orange one began, "we've gotten a report of a serious crime."

"Impossible." My voice came out shrill and much too fast. "There was no crime. You must have heard wrong. No crime whatsoever."

They looked at each other, then back at me. The orange one spoke again. "We intercepted messages between Richena Rossi and Pietro, which appeared to say that Captain Rossi kidnapped you."

Wait, what?

It hadn't crossed my mind to report the kidnapping. I'd assumed that Richena would get away with it, like she'd gotten away with everything, and I figured she'd take credit for peace on Cassiopeia VII. Now, incredibly, I could take that away and make her face the consequences of her actions, and implicate Pietro as well. For once, I was going to win. I took a breath and opened my mouth, about to tell the security officers the whole sordid story.

The plan that had been forming in my head suddenly snapped the last pieces into place. I knew how to get to the Civilizer. And in order for my plan to work, I was going to need both Richena and Pietro.

"I'm sorry, there's been a misunderstanding," I said. "There was no kidnapping. Some kidding, and possibly some napping. But no kidnapping. Sorry to take up your time." I escorted the two surprised-looking Cygnoids to the exit.

A message from Beau popped up on my beepity-beeper. *I mentioned your wrong-timeline theory to Richena, and that seemed to upset her. She wouldn't tell me why. When you get the chance, I want to talk to you about it some more.*

I grinned, but then it slid into a grimace. I had a super-weapon to destroy first.

16

Silence, Punctuated by a Violin Solo

"This looks like an interesting party." Nina walked onto the bridge of the *Turkey,* with Randy close behind her. "What's the occasion?"

I looked around the room and met a lot of skeptical faces, all here at my invitation. Randy seated himself as far as possible from me, for his own protection. Nlubglub and Adequate Leader exchanged glares. Richena kept a firm grip on Beau's arm, trying to ignore the thoughtful way he watched me. Martian tinkered with his instant-ice-rink creator. Frink reached for Lola's pocket, which was a problem, since my plan required him to have two functioning hands still attached to his body. Pietro had a notepad and an annoying smirk. And Zeeko was…Zeeko. Pilar gave me an encouraging smile.

"There's a way to get rid of the Civilizer," I began. "But it's going to require cooperation among all of us."

Pietro giggled. Lola silenced him with a look.

I turned on the viewscreen and put up the pictures of the TV building. "We've all tried to break in. We've all failed, and the Cygnoids have upped their defenses. But we have a lot of skills in this room. We have the best engineer in GUPPEAS." I nodded at Martian. "And one of the best thieves." Frink looked around, pretending not to know what I was talking about. "We have two curling champions."

Adequate Leader's antennae straightened. "What's that got to do with the Civilizer?"

"I'll get to that. We have two people who can throw a hell of a punch." Lola and Richena looked at each other appraisingly. "We have a robot, a doctor, a reporter, and two shape-shifters."

"Two?" Richena looked around. "I see one Jupiteran."

Nina slowly morphed into the image of a Cygnoid. My crew already knew her secret, but for those who didn't, she explained, "Forty-seventh-gender Jupiteran. I can't fly like a Cygnoid, but I can look like them or any species. On Jupiter they call me the Silver Sword."

Richena squirmed. The Silver Sword was a well-known name in our solar system, and Richena had tried to take credit for her exploits.

"Oh, sure," came an irritated voice, "don't mention me."

I cleared my throat. "We have Komputer, who worked out the curling angles, and who will also be providing the background music for this meeting." A quiet string quartet piece began playing. "Here's my plan."

I explained, with illustrations and diagrams. Skeptical looks turned to expressions of hopeful determination.

"What if we accidentally set off the weapon?" Adequate Leader shuddered. "I don't ever want to get hit by that thing again."

"I'll be standing by with tranquilizers and chocolate," Pilar said.

"We'll get the Civilizer out of there," I continued, "and Martian will figure out how to deactivate it. We'll tell the Cygnoids that we have it, but won't use it if they agree to never build another one."

"And if Martian can't deactivate it," Pietro added, "we'll hand it to Janet. She'll make it explode and implode at the same time, like she did to my stereo." Nobody laughed.

I looked around again. There would be more questions, but no one was backing out. "Everyone clear?"

"Yes," Beau said. "I'm in."

Richena looked like she wanted to argue, but finally said, *"We're in,"* her eyes never leaving Beau.

"Me too." That was Adequate Leader, his antennae at attention. "I'll do whatever it takes to get rid of that horrible machine."

Other voices joined in, one after another, and the mismatched crowd on my bridge pulled together into a team.

"Wait," Zeeko said. "What am I supposed to do?"

There was a brief silence, punctuated by a violin solo.

"Stay on the ship," I told him. "If the plan goes horribly wrong, call GUPPEAS and ask for instructions."

Lola arched an eyebrow. "But what could possibly go wrong?"

We approached the TV building's front door shortly after sunset. The coast was clear, except for two guards posted on either side of the door. "The building's closed," one of them said.

Lola dropped him with a punch. Richena slammed the other against the wall. We quickly tied them up and rubber-banded their beaks shut. "You'll be fine," Pilar assured the guards before we dragged them to a spot hidden behind the tree's giant roots. They didn't look convinced.

When I turned around, there was a uniformed Cygnoid guard behind me.

The scream got caught in my throat. I clamped it down when I saw the aqua eyes. "Nina," I whispered, "warn us when you're going to do that."

"Sorry," she whispered. She took a captured guard's stun gun. Martian used their keys to deactivate the alarm and unlock the door.

Grebe was sitting at the front desk in the lobby, selfies smiling down from the wall. I peered in the window, straining to listen as Pietro approached him.

"Hi, the guards let me in to give you some great news. My editor at the *Galactic Times* is interested in a story about the Cygnoid plans for peace. We've all heard what the Counselor has to say, but how do real people on Cygnus IV feel about it? Is it a burden, taking on the challenge of peace in the galaxy?"

Grebe sat up straighter, smoothing his wings. "It's an honor."

Pietro sat on the corner of the desk, training a camera on Grebe. "Do you think other species can be made to get along?"

"Sure. Maybe not Jupiterans and Plutonians. The best we can

hope for is they leave each other alone. But other species can be reasonable." Grebe fluffed the feathers around his face, eyes never leaving the camera. "You Venusians, for instance, once you see the possibilities for shopping and fashion when you don't have to maneuver around your neighbors' warships."

"Fashion?" Pietro's aura shimmered with delight. "Tell me more."

"Hurry up," Lola hissed, lurking next to me. I shared her frustration but didn't like the way she kept smacking her fist against her hand.

After more chatter, Pietro talked Grebe into taking selfies and moving down the hall where the light was better. When it was safe, Pietro signaled by brightening his aura, the light still visible after he and Grebe were out of sight. Martian slipped inside and reprogrammed the security cameras to show an endless loop of the building empty except for the guards making their rounds.

At a hand wave from Martian, the rest of us hurried inside and squeezed into the freight elevator. Thanks to the pictures Pietro had taken earlier, we found the shortest route to the restricted area on the twelfth floor.

When we reached the final hallway, Randy lowered his internal thermostat to room temperature and moved in front of the security device on the wall, blocking it from sensing the warmth of biological life-forms until we were all past. We had to repeat this process every three meters until we passed the last sensor at the end of the hall.

Frink pulled out his electronic lockpick and fiddled with the codes for half a minute. The door slid open. Nina stayed outside, impersonating a guard.

We entered the room with the Civilizer.

We stood along the narrow catwalk along the sides of the room, the only solid floor. The tangle of branches that served as a floor for the rest of the room looked less sturdy than I remembered. At the far end, almost distant enough for a curling rink, lay the nest surrounded by the laser web, each laser stopping a few centimeters above the branches to keep from frying them. And in the center of that, a device no larger than a curling stone, yet powerful enough to keep the whole galaxy in terror of humiliation.

Martian set down his latest invention and hit a button. The air shimmered and went dry as the water vapor was pulled out of it. A grid of lights appeared on the floor as Martian's device measured the room, then covered it in a smooth layer of ice, a millimeter below the laser web.

"Ambassador and Adequate Leader," I said, "you're up."

Adequate Leader set down the curling stone, and Beau positioned his broom. Beau told Nlubglub, "Ready when you are."

Nlubglub moved to the far end of the room and curled a tentacle through the web, gently reaching toward the Civilizer. "This is as close as I can get." They wobbled for a moment, almost touching a laser, then steadied.

"Careful," Pilar said nervously. "If you stretch too far—"

"I can do it," Nlubglub said. "Hurry."

Outside the door, I heard Nina speaking loudly. "No one's allowed in here!" There were other voices, but I couldn't make them out.

Nlubglub looked at Beau and spoke softly. "Three…two…one… go."

Adequate Leader slid the stone, and then Beau ran beside it, sweeping a path along the ice. Longtime habit from years of curling kept him from touching the stone itself. He stopped at the edge of the laser web, and the stone slid through.

I looked around, fearful that other new security features had escaped our notice. The cameras stayed off, the viewscreen was dark, and no alarms sounded. The voices outside faded away.

The stone hit the pressure plate just right. It slid on, knocking the Civilizer toward Nlubglub, who cradled it in their tentacle. They carefully retracted through the web, back to the catwalk, sliding the Civilizer along. Once it was outside the lasers, Nlubglub handed it over to Martian.

"That was awesome," Martian said. "Let's go. I can't wait to take this apart."

We'd done it. Captured the weapon that had held us all in terror.

And despite my technology jinx, nothing had gone wrong.

Randy wobbled and bumped into me. "I shouldn't have kept my body temperature down that long. Starting to overheat." He stumbled forward, toward the rink. The ice sizzled and melted away, raining on whatever was below us. The branches shook.

Beau and Adequate Leader flung themselves back toward us to keep from falling through. Nlubglub nearly dropped between the branches, but grabbed the edge of the catwalk and pulled themself up.

Melting ice tipped the nest with the curling stone. The stone slid off the pressure plate and disappeared into a gap between branches.

Alarms blared from every side, and force fields blocked the doors.

17

Level Zero

A force field disappeared as the Counselor entered with a half dozen Cygnoid guards, including the two we'd left tied up outside. They had their particle guns trained on Pietro, Nina (still in Cygnoid guise, but disarmed), and a confused-looking Zeeko.

Or maybe I was the one who looked confused. "Zeeko? What are you doing here?"

Zeeko smiled, as if he'd run into us on the street. "I called GUPPEAS like you told me. They said to come here and get you."

"I said to only call them if the plan went horribly wrong."

"Right." He shrugged. "I figured it would. Didn't it?"

"Well...yes, but..."

One of the guards trained their gun on Martian. "Give it back." I knew Martian well enough to understand the calculation he was making: could he figure out how to use the Civilizer faster than the Cygnoid could fire?

He couldn't. He handed over the Civilizer.

The Counselor cleared his throat. He had that "We're not mad, just disappointed" look that I'd come to dread. "I see that you haven't learned. We'll have to show you what the Civilizer can do on Level Zero."

I eyed the exit. So close, and so unreachable. "There's a Level Zero?"

"Yes. We thought the worst we could do was make you relive the most humiliating moment of your life. Then we discovered we could pull the memory out of your head and broadcast it so that everyone else could see it too."

The thought was too horrifying. Reliving that moment, with Richena and Pietro able to see it? And Beau?

"I don't think so." Lola's aura was the red of molten lava. "Maybe you hadn't noticed, but there's more of us than you."

Richena removed her earrings and pocketed them. "And if you're going to broadcast someone's memories, you can't hit more than one of us at a time. No one's going to be looking at other people's memories while they're reliving their own." She took a menacing step toward the Cygnoids.

"Uh, we're from a peace organization," Beau said.

"I'm not." Adequate Leader raised his broom like a club.

A Cygnoid guard aimed a gun at him. "Good thing we have these."

"No need for that," the Counselor said with a smirk. "Set the Civilizer back to Level One, and we can hit all of them at once."

A still-woozy Randy pulled himself to his feet as his communicator chirped. The message included both audio and letters appearing in the air. *Incoming from Cassiopeia VII. Galactic Military ships have departed Cassiopeia system and are headed this way.*

"That might be a problem for everyone here on the planet," I said. With the conflict on Cassiopeia resolved, the fleet could get here faster than a GUPPEAS bureaucrat could ask for a report in triplicate.

The Counselor pulled out a communicator. "Grebe, did you get the security cameras fixed? Good. We'll give the military ships a demonstration of what the Civilizer can do. Starting with our guests here."

Randy still had the communicator on, and a new message appeared. *Jupiteran and Plutonian Divisions of the Galactic Fleet will be the first to arrive.*

The Counselor gave a mocking laugh. "They'll be too busy shooting at each other to bother with us."

Beau looked at him in dismay. "Isn't that what you said you were trying to prevent?"

Despite all their moral posturing, I could see that the Cygnoids enjoyed the power that their weapon gave them, the ability to use other people's worst moments for their own entertainment. And if we stopped them with violence, the Cygnoids would fight back, and it would get worse and worse and spiral out of control.

Everything about this was wrong. I'd tried so hard, made such a good plan, gotten people who hated each other to work together.

Wait a minute.

"Stop!" I said, as the Cygnoids aimed their evil weapon. "Don't you see that you've succeeded?"

The Counselor gave me a blank look. "Succeeded?"

Pietro raised his camera and started filming.

I told the Counselor, "You wanted us all to stop fighting each other. That was the whole point of your peace conference, right? And look who you brought together to stop you. Jupiterans and Plutonians on the same team—who would have thought that was possible? Ursans and Venusians. Humans and anyone."

"She sorta has a point," said one of the Cygnoids.

"Shut up," said another.

"Obviously, this was your plan all along," Beau told the Counselor, forcing a smile.

"My...plan...?"

"You have two choices," I said. "You can keep trying to defend this machine, make everyone miserable when you use it, and try to hold off the Galactic Military, which will soon include robots who are immune to your weapon. You can look forward to the day when someone else builds a worse version of the Civilizer and turns it on you."

"I have some ideas for that," Martian said.

I elbowed him and kept talking to the Cygnoids. "Or you can take the win and be galactic heroes. They'll make all kinds of documentaries about you and your success in bringing everyone together against the Civilizer, so that it would never be used again."

"You'll get your own TV series," Nina said. "It'll win all kinds of awards. Even the one shaped like a sliced-up banana."

Seeing the Counselor hesitate, I added, "This is the part where you say something wise-sounding, like, 'The real Civilizer was inside you all along.'"

Beau's face brightened. "How about, 'The real Civilizer is the friends we make along the way'?"

I smiled at Beau. "Even better."

The Cygnoids looked at each other, and back at the crowd of assorted species. The Counselor cleared his throat and looked straight into Pietro's camera. "Right. Um. The real Civilizer is the friends we make along the way."

We all cheered as loudly as we could, before the Counselor could change his mind. Pietro hit a button sending the film to his editor.

I pulled out my beepity-beeper. I wanted to be the one to call GUPPEAS, before Richena found a way to make herself the hero again.

The beepity-beeper wouldn't turn on. I hit the button again, and shook the device a couple of times. Sometimes that worked, but not today. I smacked it hard against my palm.

The back panel of the beepity-beeper broke off and went flying across the room. It hit the Civilizer and knocked the control lever down to Level Zero. I heard the buzz as it powered up.

It was pointed at me.

It took a fraction of a second for me to absorb what was happening. A fraction of a fraction of a second for me to dive out of the way.

Not fast enough.

The room faded away, but not entirely. The viewscreens on every wall lit up with an image that I'd tried to forget...

I found myself back at Kappa Leporis III, my second assignment with GUPPEAS.

The Leporines, from the constellation Lepus, were a little-known species. There had been a few unofficial contacts, but this was the first diplomatic overture from GUPPEAS. My ship's computer didn't have much information on the species, but there was one important diplomatic protocol: Before anyone spoke, the Leporine leader was to be kissed on the mouth. By the commander of the vessel. Me.

I hadn't kissed very many people in my life: Pietro, Beau, a couple of high school boyfriends. According to Pietro, I wasn't very good at it. Beau hadn't ventured an opinion, and I couldn't ask, since it had happened in the alternate timeline that he didn't know about.

When the ship touched down, a party of Leporines met us at the landing site. They looked like bipedal slugs in a dark bluish-brown color, each with an enormous, slimy-looking mouth. The crew and I walked down the ramp. I went up to the lead alien and planted a smooch on one very surprised Leporine.

"Gross!" The Leporine jumped back and spat in a very messy way, dark brown goo all over my shoes.

"Ew, do we have to do that?" one of the other Leporines said. "Doesn't your species have any concept of personal space? Boundaries?"

"But—but—but—" I looked around, sputtering. "My computer said that this was how your species showed respect."

Through the still-open hatch behind us, Komputer was howling with laughter.

I took a step forward, trying to explain myself, and slipped on the Leporine slime all over my shoes. I fell toward the alien leader, who thought I was attempting another kiss and jumped back with a shriek.

I tried to wrench myself out of the memory, back into the present. It had turned out all right: we'd explained it as an unfortunate miscommunication, and the Leporines eventually agreed not to declare war. I'd gotten my revenge on the computer later, by pressing its buttons until it had an hours-long sneezing fit.

But now I was back in that moment, drowning in shame as I realized I'd become the face of GUPPEAS to an entire species. Wishing I was anywhere else in the universe. A dungeon on Pluto. The surface of the sun. Anywhere.

The computer's laughter echoed in my head, and its smug voice: "I was going to tell you the Leporines were offended by other species wearing clothes, but I didn't think you'd believe it. I should have gone for it!"

Pilar's voice pulled me back into the present. "The tranquilizer will take effect soon. It's all right, Captain. Take this chocolate, and concentrate on—"

Even chocolate couldn't ease my horror. The kiss was replaying on the viewscreen in slow motion. I turned away and my gaze focused on the so-called Civilizer. I leapt forward, yanking it out of the Counselor's hands. My shaking fingers fumbled with the controls, trying desperately to turn it off.

The beam spun wildly, and struck Richena.

Another image took over the viewscreen.

I recognized the scene. Richena and I were both there, along with Beau, my crew, and a roomful of Plutonians. We were on an impossible mission, on a planet where chocolate was illegal. I was tired, cranky, scared, and chocolate-deprived. And then Exalted Leader canceled the ban on chocolate, and in a moment of giddy exuberance, I kissed the most amazing man I'd ever met. Beau.

It was strange, watching Richena's memory, seeing myself through her eyes. I saw how enthusiastically Beau was kissing back.

Beau and Richena were in one of their many breakups at the time, but they'd had to hide it because of Plutonian politics. A hiss escaped through Richena's teeth as everyone watched her supposed soulmate kissing someone less beautiful, less successful, just plain *less* than she was.

Richena, an accomplished captain for a peace organization, lost her cool and threw me across the room. In the light Plutonian gravity, I flew out the door.

The viewscreen captured it all: the moment when Beau's surprise at the kiss turned to pleasure, the Plutonians looking aghast, the utter disinterest of Exalted Leader because, hello, *chocolate*. Richena caught her reflection in one of the metal cabinets, her teeth bared with rage.

And now everyone could see it. My face burned. I couldn't look at Beau.

His voice was calm but puzzled: "That never happened."

I couldn't find the words.

Pilar spoke up. "Then why does Richena look so mad about it?"

I looked over at Richena. She was red-faced, her eyes shooting lasers at me.

I steadied myself and pushed the viewscreen's images out of my brain. "It happened in an alternate reality. Richena used her time-travel shuttle to alter the timeline. She changed a few other things, too. You broke up with her. There's a reason you keep putting off giving her that ring. I believe that on some level, you sensed the timeline shift. Some part of you still remembers."

"That's ridiculous!" Richena snarled.

Beau looked from her to me, and the expression on his face moved from doubt to trust. Unexpectedly, by facing that awful moment, I'd brought the truth out.

He brushed past Richena and came to stand in front of me. "Tell me about this other timeline. All of it."

And then I couldn't answer, because he was kissing me again.

Rugworm Tea for Plutherxib

On our way home, we stopped at Buck's Star, a place that defies all laws of physics by always being nearby. Buck's Star is known for having more kinds of coffee than anywhere else in the universe. The crew and I wound up in a café filled with aliens, all busy with their communication devices. Out the window, we could see an endless line of spaceships waiting at the drive-through.

"Double mocha for Jam-it," called the barista.

"Seriously, Jam-it? Do they read Pietro's column here too?"

"They get everyone's name wrong." Nlubglub held up a full cup labeled *Noseslug*. "It's practically a tradition."

"Wait, you don't drink—"

"I like the aroma." Nlubglub sprouted three noses. "And it helps me fit in with the rest of the crew. Shape-shifters like to fit in."

"Hot chocolate for Blue," said the barista.

"That's mine." Beau got up, and I followed him to the counter.

On the way back, he told me, "We would have gotten to Cassiopeia VII sooner, but Frink detoured us to Rigel before anyone realized what he was doing. You know about his long-distance relationship with a Rigelian who ghosted him? Anyway, he couldn't find them— they supposedly ran a shop, but the address was empty."

"Think he'll stop stealing wedding rings now?"

"Probably not."

We returned to the table as the barista called, "Triple espresso for

Mashup."

Martian wrinkled his nose. "Mashup? Oh come on, they're not even trying. I should tell them the story of how I got my name."

As Martian walked away, Beau said, "I always meant to ask him about his name."

Everyone at the table spoke simultaneously: "Don't."

The rest of the crew returned to reading their beepity-beeper screens. Pilar was texting with her kids about their plans after college, and strongly advising them against joining GUPPEAS. Frink was reading something that had him chuckling. "You don't want to see Pietro's column," he said.

The announcement came: "Cappuccino for Lolagnya og de Thurwolliger."

I looked at Lola in surprise. "They got your full name right?"

"I told them what would happen if they didn't." Lola went to get her drink.

Pietro's column was more or less what I'd expected.

I don't want to overstate my heroics, but I can safely say that the Counselor's evil plan to conquer the galaxy couldn't have been defeated without me. Due credit also to the amazing Richena Rossi, fresh off her victory over the robot uprising on Cassiopeia VII.

The accompanying picture of Pietro and Richena looked very cozy.

Lola returned, eyes on her beepity-beeper screen. "The first episode of Grebe's reality show isn't bad. They've got the Counselor putting people through ridiculous tasks. Winner gets to be the next Counselor."

"I'm glad to be out of there," I said. "When we crash-landed, I thought things couldn't get worse from there, but they did. Sometimes it felt like everything under that double sun was unlucky or, I don't know..."

"Star-crossed?" Beau knew exactly how to finish my sentence.

I raised my coffee cup. "To the star-crossed Pelican Nebula. May we not have to go back there for a good long time." Beau and I drank a toast.

Two audio messages arrived simultaneously on my beepity-beeper, and the voices got mixed up so that it took me a moment to sort out which one was Nina and which was my mother.

"We heard about your accomplishments on Cygnus IV, and we're very proud of you both. We're back on Lyra II, finally getting shore leave. Hope to see you there soon."

"Robotics have advanced further than I'd realized. Turns out Randy can live almost as long as a Jupiteran. Anyway, we're going dancing tonight."

The barista called, "Rugworm tea for Plutherxib." Zeeko got up and headed for the counter.

"Bring Martian back with you," Lola called after him. "Or he'll talk the barista's ear off."

I scrutinized the picture with Pietro's column. His aura was a blindingly cheerful purple. "You don't think that Pietro and Richena…"

Beau chuckled. "I'd stay out of the crossfire when that combination blows up. Neither of them can handle being anything but the center of attention."

"Hazelnut Frappuccino for Felon." The twelve-armed barista sounded harried. "And chai bacon latte for…I dunno, something with a whole lot of X's and Z's."

Frink arrived at the counter at the same time as a Rigelian. The Rigelian wore a diamond ring on each of their twenty fingers.

I was distracted by a call on the beepity-beeper from Vertin Bogler, my superior at GUPPEAS.

"Hello, Captain." His smarmy green aura seemed to radiate through the screen. "After your recent successes on Pluto and Cygnus, I'm sure your new assignment will be an excellent use of your skills."

"Assignment? There's no assignment." I glanced at Lola, who looked ready to smash things if our shore leave got delayed again. "You told us we have leave time coming."

"There's an emergency. Wait, are you at Buck's Star? On your way back, could you bring me a large half-caf, half-whole-milk, half-clobberfruit-milk, gourd-spice latte?"

Beau asked, "You said there was an emergency?"

"Oh yes. The Plutonians are threatening to riot over chocolate deprivation."

"We already took care of that," I said. "Chocolate is no longer banned, remember?"

"Of course. But some fool introduced the Vegans to chocolate, and they invaded Pluto and ate all the chocolate there. Now they're threatening to eat the Plutonians."

Nlubglub snorted through all three noses. "Works for me."

Frink returned with his arm around the Rigelian. "Everyone, this is Xerxzez, they and them. It turns out they were looking for me the whole time I was looking for them."

"Pleasure to meet you all." Xerxzez had a musical voice that ping-ponged back and forth from high notes to low ones. It took a moment to remember where I'd heard it before. *We have been trying to reach you about the extended warranty for your spaceship...*

I decided Frink and Xerxzez were going to work out fine.

Bogler droned on, "There may be a slight difficulty with the fact that GUPPEAS uniforms are the same colors as the wrapper for a popular Vegan snack cake."

Lola's aura turned a bloody red. "I say we take that leave time on Lyra, whether GUPPEAS likes it or not."

There were murmurs of agreement around the table. I tried to turn off the beepity-beeper, but the button was stuck.

Bogler continued, "We'll need to fill the ship with chocolate for the mission in all available storage space, including crew quarters."

Beau and I spoke simultaneously: "We'll be right there."

About the Author

Laura Ruth Loomis is a social worker by day, space cadet by night. She writes contemporary fiction as well as science fiction and fantasy. Her contemporary chapbook of linked short stories, *Lost in Translation*, is available from Wordrunner Press. Her fiction and nonfiction have appeared in *Writer's Digest, The Saturday Evening Post, On the Premises, Prime Number, Women on Writing*, and elsewhere.

The Cosmic Turkey series had its genesis in middle school, when Laura would write stories to keep herself entertained. Decades later, when she was stuck on other writing projects, she thought back to a time when writing was pure fun, and the *Turkey* flew once more.

Laura lives in Northern California, with her wife, Terry, their assorted pets, and possibly a Plutonian saboteur who keeps stealing their socks.

Acknowledgements

Thanks to the writers, readers, and editors who help me get Janet's adventures from daydream to book form: Aline Soules (curling consultant), Dean Gloster (coffee expert), Dennis Cusack, Karen Schwabach, and Laura "Classic" Remington. Special thanks to Stephanie Carr for more than 20 years of reading and writing together—I hope someday you teach me your secret for having your characters' voices so pitch perfect every time.

Thanks to the amazing people at Thinklings Books, especially awesome editors Deborah Jeanne Natelson and Sarah Awa, and cover artist Nada Orlic.

Thanks to my parents, Jim and Mary Loomis, for a lifetime of encouragement. Thanks to my brother, Patrick Loomis, still the original Martian (and probably the only other person who knows the story behind the song "Your Love Is Like a Cold Slice of Pizza"). Thanks to my nieces, Jennifer Marshall and Grace Silva, my favorite target audience.

First, last, and always, thanks to my wife, Terry Silva, for being the love of my life in this timeline and any other.

Thinklings
TIMELESS BOOKS • QUALITY AUTHORS

www.ThinklingsBooks.com
Facebook.com/ThinklingsBooks
@ThinklingsBooks

Thinklings Books started out when three speculative-fiction-loving professional editors—Deborah Natelson, Sarah Awa, and Jeannie Ingraham—got together and formed a writing group. We called ourselves the Thinklings, in honor of C.S. Lewis and J.R.R. Tolkien's group, the Inklings.

Over time, we found ourselves agonizing more and more about how messed-up the publishing industry had become. Why couldn't good books get published? Why were so many bad books published just because their authors had big Twitter followings? We wished there were something we could do about the problem . . . and then we realized there was.

As a developmental editor, a substantive/line editor, and a proofreader, the three of us knew good writing when we saw it—and we knew how to make it even better. We had a lot of experience walking our clients through the publishing process—both traditional and self-publish—and we had contacts with marketing and design experts. We had some amazing unpublished books lined up and ready for production. We had, in fact, everything we needed to make a great publishing company. All that was left was to actually do it.

So we're doing it.

Spectacular Reads. Every Time.

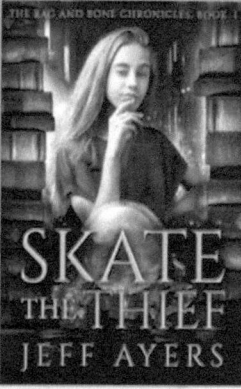

TALES OF THE MYTHUSIAN EMPIRE by Remy Apepp

One is Blessed. One is cursed. Neither is entirely sure which is which.

Endlessly attacked by accursed beings, the kingdom of Ordyuk relies ever more heavily on four siblings. Under such a weight, their only choice is to grow into monsters themselves—
Or to shatter like glass.

AND YOU THOUGHT COLLEGE WAS TOUGH BEFORE

Try getting bitten by a werewolf. And being hunted by madmen. And being stalked by a very suspicious secret organization.

Hunter's Moon by Sarah M. Awa

THE CLOCK IS TICKING

Plans seldom survive contact with the enemy, a truth thrown at Mercedes when an ordinary trip turns into a battle for survival.

Bargaining Power by Deborah J. Natelson